# CAPTURED!

The horses and their riders loomed above Nathan and his family, casting shadows like an eclipse of the sun.

"Look what's hiding here—Quakers!" The one soldier spat out the word, as though he had discovered thieves. Both soldiers sheathed their swords. "Why are you hiding here?"

Slowly Nathan stood up, holding his shaking younger brother.

"You are disloyal to the king!" the other soldier accused.

Nathan's brother ran to cling to his mother's waist.

"Dissenter!" The first soldier shouted as he dismounted. "You will come with us—all of you!"

# THE PRISONERS' SWORD

**Barbara Chamberlain**

**Illustrated by Arnie Kohn**

David C. Cook Publishing Co.

ELGIN, ILLINOIS—WESTON, ONTARIO
FULLERTON, CALIFORNIA

Published by David C. Cook Publishing Co., Elgin, IL 60120
Edited by Janet Hoover Thoma

Printed in the United States of America
Library of Congress Catalog Number 77-87256
ISBN 0-89191-102-2

# 1

NATHAN STOPPED SHORT. Something soft and squishy had hit his back. He felt the wet soaking through his coat.

Jennett stopped, too, her hands moving swiftly to his back. "It's mud, Nathan," she said in a wavering voice, as tears came to her blue eyes. "Here, let me wipe it off."

Then, from between tall houses on the narrow London street, a man's voice jeered, "Traitors!"

Nathan turned his head in the direction of the fading voice, but saw no one.

"Look straight ahead, children," Uncle Thomas ordered. "And walk quickly. We're almost home."

Nathan moved on, but his heart pounded so angrily he thought his ears would explode. If he could just grab some Londoner and scream, "Why?" Then maybe the silent strangers behind their tightly closed doors would listen.

Forgetting to watch his footing, Nathan stepped on a loose cobblestone. His worn country boot turned. The sudden pain made him wince, but he refused to limp, growing even angrier.

"I'll find out who threw that mud," he muttered. But he knew he never could.

Nathan hated the filthy streets and the smelly city of London. He wanted to erase all that had forced them to live with Uncle Thomas.

As they walked under the overhanging second stories of crowded homes, the sound of iron wheels and the "Clop, plop, clop, plop" of horses' hoofs echoed on the stones. A carriage trimmed with crimson fringe rolled by with branches of long, green leaves tied over its windows. *What did those leaves mean?* Nathan looked toward his uncle for the answer, but the man did not seem to notice the carriage or the leaves.

Nathan searched his memory, but the answer skidded into the farthest corner of his mind and hid. Nathan stared at the strangely decorated coach as they followed Uncle Thomas across the corner.

From the doorway of a house ahead, a man slipped coins into a pouch on his belt and cried, "Old clothes to buy! Anybody buy my old clothes?" Coats, shirts, and breeches hung over his arms, and he carried two old swords. Although he was shabbily dressed himself, he gave Uncle Thomas a swift, contemptuous look as they passed.

*He knows we will buy nothing,* Nathan thought, eyeing the five hats piled on the man's head, one with a long, billowy yellow feather bobbing in the breeze. The boy imagined himself wearing that hat. *Maybe if we dressed like everyone else, people would ignore us,* Nathan mused bitterly. But they had to dress in the plain Quaker fashion, making themselves targets for every coward in the city.

The blare of a ratcatcher's horn shattered Nathan's daydream. Two ratcatchers—one wearing a sash advertising his trade and the other carrying a flag picturing two rats—called, "Any rats to catch? We're the best! Let us rid your home of pests! Any work today?" The one with the horn blew it again, and paused. When no one shouted for their services, the two men moved on.

The short distance to their uncle's house seemed to stretch forever. Finally, they reached his steps. Before Nathan could press the latch, his brother Edmund opened the door from inside.

"What did you buy?" the little boy asked, looking at the sack Uncle Thomas carried.

They brushed by him. "But I'd like to see," Edmund persisted.

The aroma of a roasting joint of beef filled the house. Any other time, Nathan would have dashed straight to the fire to admire the bubbling brown fat and beg for a slice of meat. Instead, he slammed the door and stood rigid, his mind seething with revenge against their unknown tormentors.

Jennett moved to her big brother and turned him to wipe the remaining mud off his coat.

"What happened?" their mother asked as she stood up, setting her mending on the chair. Suddenly Jennett sobbed, burying her head in her mother's chest.

Nathan noticed mud clinging to the ends of her long, blond hair. So it had splattered her also! He clenched his hand into a fist and struck his palm hard. He and his ten-year-old sister had never harmed anyone. *We're not traitors!*

His mother's blue eyes clouded as their uncle explained and then added, "I think Jennett should stay in the house with you, Ellen, the next time we go shopping. I bought as much as possible today, so we won't have to go out too soon." He avoided her eyes, setting the sack of cheese, meat, apples, and cabbages on the floor. Edmund picked up a cabbage in each hand and carried them to the kitchen.

While Jennett continued to cry, Uncle Thomas seemed to delete the incident from his mind. *What would ever make him angry?* His uncle's Quaker calmness made Nathan resent their treatment even more. *Why were they persecuted like this?* They only wanted to be left in peace. But they did not worship as the king wished. For this, they were called dissenters and scorned by everyone.

"I hate London," Nathan barely muttered the words aloud. "We can't even walk the streets."

His mother turned toward him. He saw color rising in her pale cheeks. Her sorrowful blue eyes met his angry gaze.

"If there had been any way to stay on our farm in Yorkshire, we would be there now," she replied. "I will buy another farm for us if we ever receive payment for our land."

"Ellen," Thomas broke in. "You know how many letters I've written to the sheriff there, but none has been answered."

Rage boiled inside Nathan, a feeling that had burned in his heart since they had been ordered to leave their farm.

"I know you came to me for help, Ellen," Uncle Thomas continued, removing his wide-brimmed black hat and smoothing his hand over his thinning blond hair. "When you came, I was overjoyed to have you, to have children in this lonely house." He replaced his hat. "But now I know how much more content you were on the farm. I cannot seem to touch the hearts of men in power. They won't accept my letters."

When their lands had been taken, Nathan's mother had feared for their lives. She had hired a guide with a cart and brought her family to London, with as many of their belongings as possible. The children were still weak from the smallpox that had taken their father. Often on their journey, the safety and protection of their uncle's house had seemed worlds away.

11

"Your uncle tutors the sons of many royal families," their mother told them. "He will be able to help us."

But Thomas was also a Quaker, and no one was safe who belonged to the Society of Friends, as the Quakers called themselves. And the Friends made themselves obvious targets by dressing in plain gray and refusing to attend the king's church. Instead, they held their own meetings.

"I'm hungry," Edmund spoke up. "When will we eat?"

Mother wiped the tears from Jennett's eyes and brushed Nathan's coat one last time. He noticed how lines had deepened in his mother's forehead in the last few months. Dark circles hid her eyes, and her once rosy cheeks—never marked by the pox scars Thomas and other adults carried—had paled to gray white. His mother had nursed them through smallpox six months ago, when their father died. She needed to return to the country. They all did. Thomas could come, too.

"We will have dinner now, Edmund," mother promised, placing Nathan's coat over a chair. "You can't even see the spot, Nathan. Now, will you bring the trenchers to the table?"

Nathan moved unwillingly to take the heavy wooden plates from the kitchen shelf.

"Jennett, why don't you read to Edmund while I carve the roast?" Uncle Thomas suggested. The girl nodded, taking her favorite book, *Aesop's Fa-*

*bles,* from their uncle's small but precious library on his writing desk.

Carefully positioned under the real glass window to catch the best light, the writing desk was the first one the children had seen. They had expected Londoners to have fine furniture. But a desk just for writing! This one was well-used, because their uncle wrote continually about their faith to Friends in many cities.

Edmund snuggled beside Jennett. She had read almost every book from the neatly stacked, leather-bound volumes. Jennett was content in a corner with a book, while some days Nathan felt his own rage would explode. Nathan's God—no longer the quiet spirit of his mother, uncle, and other Friends—marched with the roar of the God of Israel's armies long ago, destroying enemies with fury. How Nathan wished for that power, the mighty power of a brave soldier. He knew his feelings were different from those of his family. . . .

"Come to the table," their mother called.

Nathan slipped last onto the wooden bench, resting his elbow on the table and leaning his chin in his hand. He stared at the floor while his uncle cut a portion of beef and slipped it onto his trencher with the end of the knife. Nathan turned his aching foot from side to side under the table.

"Mother made a rabbit pie, Nate," Edmund said, as he sliced the beef with his meat knife and grabbed a steaming piece with his fingers.

13

"Ouch!" he dropped the meat and blew on his burned hand.

"Patience, Edmund," Uncle Thomas cautioned, placing a slice of pie on the little boy's trencher.

Nathan cut a tiny slice of meat, spearing it with the tip of his knife and lifting the meat to his mouth. The warm fat ran over the knife's hilt onto his hand, cooling and becoming solid on his wrist. His stomach burned as he chewed the hot beef.

"May I leave the table, mother?" he asked.

"Please sit with us until dinner is finished," she replied after glancing at Uncle Thomas. Nathan had known what she would say. Why had he bothered to ask?

The boy watched little Edmund consume enough for three people, while each piece of meat stuck in his own throat. Usually he could devour a whole rabbit pie himself, but he left the slice on his trencher untouched.

At last his uncle rose, "A delicious meal, Ellen. While the children wipe the trenchers, I will write another letter to the sheriff in Yorkshire about your lands."

Nathan knew that no answer would ever come.

"Children," Uncle Thomas added, "we'll have your lessons as soon as I finish this letter."

*How can he call me a child when I'm already as tall as he is?* Nathan watched as his uncle smoothed the sheet of parchment, carefully turning it slightly to the left to pen his flowing script.

He dipped the quill repeatedly in ink, wiping the tip carefully to avoid blotting. The feather tip danced with each stroke of his uncle's hand.

*He should have left the feather on the goose for all the good it does,* Nathan thought bitterly. They needed someone to take action, not just write letters.

"I'm ready for my lesson, uncle," broke in Edmund as he positioned his hornbook on his lap. "I like learning my letters. When I learn all my lessons, I shall be rich. Then I will be a duke and ride in a grand carriage with a driver and footman. No, maybe three footmen." He held up three fingers and counted them. "The footmen will walk ahead of my coach and cry, 'Here comes Edmund Cowell. Make way for his carriage!' And I shall own the most beautiful horses in England."

"Edmund, you cannot be wealthy or a duke, either!" Nathan snapped.

The boy stepped back, as though his brother had hit him, and ran to Jennett.

"Let him dream, Nathan," Jennett scolded. "He's only five."

"Let him hear the truth," Nathan bristled. "We cannot do anything, because we are Friends and do not worship as the king wishes. We cannot hold public office, and our lands are stolen by greedy men."

"That is enough, Nathan." There could be no mistaking the firm tone of his mother's voice. "You

15

and Edmund and Jennett will begin your lessons now!"

A resigned sigh escaped the boy's lips. "All right, mother. But if all our Friends from every meeting in England joined together, we could build our own city and rule it. Then everyone would have to obey us."

"Then we would rule as the king does," Thomas answered. "What would be the difference?"

*"We* would tell everyone what to do."

"You and your friends would rule. Here the king and his friends rule. I see no difference. Why not build a city where men who are the most capable rule, whether they are Quakers or not?"

Nathan frowned. Here the world melted around them like a cheap tallow candle while they argued about their dreams. The king ruled England.

Uncle Thomas gathered his books. "We must begin before the day slips by."

Today his uncle's lesson was lost to him. Usually Nathan daydreamed through most of it, anyway, while Jennett absorbed every word.

Looking across the room, he wondered why his mother was again mending his uncle's coat. He did not remember any rips or tears in it. Now Nathan realized that she was not mending the coat, but carefully sewing coins into its lining. She had sewn coins into their clothes once before, when they came to London. He interrupted his uncle's grammar lesson.

"Mother, are we—" Nathan stopped in the middle of his question, his heart echoing a sudden pounding at their door. Too late, he saw the bolt was not fastened.

Thomas looked intently at the door, and Jennett instinctively reached out for Edmund. In almost one motion, his mother slipped a small pouch of coins into the chair and rolled up his uncle's coat, dropping it on top of the money.

They all heard what they now feared most: a frantic knocking shook the front entrance of their house.

# 2

NONE OF THEM had been watching the street, so no one knew if the person on the step were an enemy. Nathan's body tensed. Because the front door was the only exit, they were trapped. His uncle already had his hand on the latch.

As Thomas opened the door slowly, Nathan relaxed. Two Quaker men entered the house. Isaac Hibbs held the top of his hat as he bent slightly to come through the door, followed by Miles Walton. Nathan knew the men from Friends' meetings. The two answered their family's welcome flatly.

"May we speak with you privately?" Isaac asked with an intent frown on his broad face.

"Let me stay," Nathan begged. His uncle nodded. Mother sent Jennett and Edmund upstairs. Nathan did not know why, because his sister and brother could easily hear their conversation. He often overheard his mother and uncle talking as he tried to fall asleep at night.

"Tell us why you came, Friends," Thomas asked.

Isaac replied quickly, "I mentioned an outbreak

of smallpox at our meeting yesterday, Thomas."

"Yes. I remember. Is it spreading?"

"It's not pox," Miles spoke gravely. "It's the plague! Some poor souls in the waterfront houses have already died."

Nathan saw fear flash in his uncle's and mother's eyes. His own arms chilled at the mention of the death word. A touch of plague—those hideous sores often meant death, in a few hours or a few days.

"As word spreads, hundreds will flee the city," Isaac warned. "Some families are already packing."

"I know." Thomas sat down at his desk and rested his forehead on his hands. "The curse before— the hellfire that followed." Nathan knew Thomas's young wife had sickened with the plague during a wave of the black death fifteen years earlier. Much of London burned then. Uncle Thomas thought the fire helped kill the plague.

"We ministered to the dying during those months. So many died." Thomas closed his eyes and shivered. "We carried countless bodies to the lime pits for burial. Only Quakers would go into some of the stricken streets."

"Miles and I are warning our friends to go to the country, if they wish to be safe," Isaac told them.

"Where?" Thomas asked. "Where can we go? Ellen and I have already thought of leaving, because of the persecution."

Nathan silently dreamed of the country.

"Any inland area is safer," Miles suggested.

Thomas rose. "Ellen, London may soon be in chaos. Taking the children away, even for a short time, will be best."

*Leave London!* Nathan had his wish.

"Prepare a pack for each of us to carry. Blankets, all the food we have. . . . Oh, I wish I owned a carriage. When I return, we will leave."

"Return?" Nathan's mother asked. "Where are you going, Thomas?"

"I'll be of what help I can today," Thomas answered. "We'll leave tomorrow morning." Isaac and Miles nodded.

They all seemed to be going to the plague area! Thomas had changed the other men's minds. Had he lost his? How could his uncle consider leaving when they needed him? He might catch the plague.

"I know how you feel, Thomas," Nathan's mother agreed. "But I must stay with my children." She gave him a brief hug. "May God be with you all."

"I thought you were going to warn other Friends," Nathan reminded Isaac.

"There are two more families close by. Will you warn them for us, Nathan?" the big man asked. "Then we will be able to help Thomas right now."

"Why do you want to help people you don't know?" Nathan questioned. "Who would help us if we were sick?" He answered himself. "Some of the Friends, if they were able. Everyone else despises us." He found his voice growing louder.

"Not everyone," Thomas offered. "Although, it often seems so. But I would never leave the city without first trying to help. My conscience would not allow it."

"Are you wearing your pomander, Thomas?" Nathan's mother cautioned him. "You forget so often."

Thomas drew out the small bag from under his shirt. "You see, Ellen, I'm not as helpless as you imagine." He turned to Isaac and Miles. "How often my younger sister pretends to be my mother. She will not allow you to leave this house unless you have yours, Friends."

Nathan felt for the spicy pomander, which was used to ward off illness, hanging around his own neck. He liked its scent, especially when they walked the foul-smelling city streets.

"My wife made me a fresh one of herbs two days ago," Isaac said.

"I never go outside without mine," Miles assured mother.

"I have two red kerchiefs in my chest upstairs. Let me fetch them." Mother lifted her skirts slightly to walk up the stairs.

Nathan remembered his father lying in bed with red curtains drawn all around. The expensive bed hangings had not saved him. Red would drive away illness—everyone knew that—but it had not worked.

Edmund and Jennett met their mother at the top of the stairs, holding the red cloths.

"Edmund! Jennett!" Mother scolded. "You were listening."

After a pause, Edmund admitted, "A little."

"All right, I know voices skip right up these stairs. You may come down and bid your uncle and our friends good-bye."

Nathan hung back while Jennett, followed by Edmund, hugged each of the men. "May God be with you," Jennett said.

As the door closed behind them, Nathan frowned. "Mother, why does Uncle Thomas waste the time? We should help ourselves."

"Thomas told us his conscience would trouble him forever if he left without trying to help. He will take us to the country in the morning, Nathan. You should have given him one kind word."

"I don't understand."

"Someday you will," she called as Nathan left to deliver his warnings. "Jennett and Edmund, help me prepare for our journey."

As he hurried along the side of the street, Nathan limped a little. Then, realizing his ankle did not hurt so much, he ran, giving Londoners less time to jeer at his gray coat and pants. How he enjoyed feeling the wind against his ears! But

"Are you home, Matt?

worry blocked his feeling of freedom. *I should have told mother to bolt the door. I'll go back soon and help her.*

Nathan warned the Hayhurst family and then dashed to the Crispin's. He liked Matt Crispin, a boy his own age. But they saw each other only at meetings, because they could not go out alone any more. As Nathan jumped up the front step, he heard a child crying inside. He pulled the ring in the brass lion's head and pounded on the door. Now all was quiet behind the shuttered window.

Nathan hit the door with the side of his fist. He noticed the door of the house next to the Crispin's open for a brief second, and then slam shut. He could not help glaring back for a moment, long enough to notice the unnatural silence that engulfed the street.

Then he remembered how they had felt when Isaac and Miles pounded on their door.

"Matt!" he cried. "Are you home? It's Nathan Cowell. Open up!" The wooden opening swung back slowly, and Matt stood before him. Startled by the boy's tearstained face, Nathan rocked back, almost falling off the step.

"Have you heard of the sickness already?" Nathan blurted out. He saw Matt's three younger sisters crying. "What's wrong? Is someone ill?"

"Nathan," Matt cried, "we need help." He drew in his breath. "My father didn't come home last night."

# 3

MATT'S WORDS STUNNED NATHAN.

"My father left to search for work yesterday and never returned," Matt explained. "I should have gone with him. But he told me I must care for my mother and sisters." Fresh tears clouded the boy's eyes.

Matt's mother appeared from the kitchen. Hannah Crispin looked at him with a colorless face. Nathan feared that the tiny woman might faint.

"Did he go toward the riverfront?" Nathan was almost afraid to ask.

"We don't know," Matt's mother shook her head. "We don't know. . . ." she repeated hopelessly.

"And who will care if one Quaker is missing?" Matt spoke bitterly. "The government may even be responsible!"

Nathan shivered, knowing his friend's words could be true. There had to be some way to help the

Crispins. "Would you go to my uncle's house?" He knew his mother and Jennett would comfort them. The Crispins would hear about the plague soon enough, so he did not say any more about the rumors.

"Do you have any food?" Nathan asked.

"A little," Matt's mother answered.

"Pack all you can carry and your blankets. . . . And, Matt, leave a note for your father."

Hannah and Matt Crispin nodded in agreement.

"I'll find my uncle," Nathan continued. "He's with Isaac Hibbs and Miles Walton. They will look for your father." The family brightened at his words and were packing as he left.

Nathan sped across Fleet Street toward the Thames River. He was annoyed that Matt sat in the house when there was an emergency. Nathan would have gone right out to search. Matt must learn to be more of a man, especially if his father. . . . The wailing notes of someone playing a pipe filled the street, and he heard laughter coming from a coffeehouse. Either news of the plague had not reached here, or Isaac and Miles had heard a false alarm.

Nathan deliberately crossed to the other side of the street to avoid a man wearing a white silk suit who was bellowing at his servant.

"I shall beat you later!" The man clutched the gilded hilt of his sword. "Or would you rather die? If we miss that coach, I shall beat you three times

26

and leave you to the plague!" The servant struggled forward with two enormous bags. So the plague was real. . . .

The clatter of wheels echoed ahead of him. Quickly, Nathan backed under the overhang of a house to avoid the racing carriage. Branches of leaves hung over the coach's windows. At last, Nathan remembered. *Leaves of rue. Leaves of the bitter herb to protect travelers from the plague.*

Nathan wondered if he might bring some rue leaves back to his family. But he had no money, not one penny. All the rue would be sold by now, anyway. Any remedies for plague were surely gleaned from the apothecary's shelves, like a field picked clean after reaping.

The thought of sweet-smelling, newly cut grain made him even more aware of the rancid odor of the streets and the frightened Londoners who rushed by him. His shoulders were bumped by men, women, and children who hastened to escape the river area. Many families were still packing their wagons. The doors of a few houses were wide open, as though the occupants had run out to escape a swift-moving fire.

For once, he felt invisible. No one seemed to notice his plain gray clothing. Today, they had more to fear than Quakers. But instead of enjoying this freedom, Nathan felt lost. He had never been alone on the streets before. Which way should he go? Dare he ask?

Even the shopkeepers were deserting their stalls and stores. In front of the cheese shop where his uncle traded, the vendor was rapidly loading a cart. The man had never treated them with contempt, as some other merchants did. Nathan wondered why he was working alone.

"May I help you pack?" he asked.

The busy man nodded, not missing a step in his rush to get out of town. Nathan followed him, loading rounds of cheese until the cart would hold no more.

The shopkeeper paused to wipe his hands on his apron and muttered a hurried thank you. "My helpers ran off," he explained. "I'll not have them back when the plague's gone. Why aren't you leaving London?"

"I'm looking for my uncle," Nathan answered.

"The two streets closest to the water are the worst. The sickness loves water. The place is cursed. . . . Son, you're not thinking of going there?" The man wiped sweat from his brow, shaking his head as he added, "Not much help can be given those down there." He slipped his hand under his coat and drew something out. "This hare's foot will bring you luck."

Nathan shook his head. "I can't take your lucky piece."

"I'm going to my cousin's in the country, where hares are everywhere," the man said. "I can get another one."

"I know," the boy answered wistfully.

"Besides," the man continued, "I'll sell this cheese for twice what it's worth. That will be luck enough for me." He sliced a large chunk of creamy white cheese and placed it and the rabbit's foot into Nathan's hands.

Clutching the foot for good luck, Nathan turned to leave. "Thank you," he called. He nibbled a corner of the cheese, then slipped it between his coat and shirt.

After looking down only two more corners, Nathan spotted Isaac's tall frame, then his uncle, and finally Miles. Maybe lucky charms did work.

Breathlessly, Nathan caught up with them.

"Nathan!" Thomas turned and stopped. "What are you doing here?"

The boy tried to breath deeply, gasping, "Henry Crispin's disappeared. He's been gone all night. . . ." He paused to take another breath. "I sent his family to mother. They are so upset. Uncle Thomas, we must find out what happened to him!"

"I'm glad you sent them to Ellen." His uncle's compliment cheered the boy.

"Where will we look?" Nathan asked.

"Nathan, how can we?"

"I promised Matt!"

Isaac put his big hand on the boy's shoulder. "The four of us couldn't possibly search all of London. Most likely Henry came down here looking for work." Nathan knew the men were right. London must be the biggest city in the world.

"I've even heard of some arrests," Miles revealed, and then stopped, his eyes darting from Nathan's surprised gaze to Isaac and Thomas. The expression on the other men's faces told Nathan that Miles's words were true. *Arrests!* Any man could be arrested for not following the state religion.

"These rumors are always with us." Thomas tried to sound casual, but it was too late. Nathan followed as the men continued toward the waterfront. He would not go back and admit they were not searching for Matt's father!

"May I stay with you?" Nathan asked. After all, he was almost as tall as his uncle, and certainly could be as brave. "I'll look for Henry Crispin as we go. Please, uncle."

"You won't like what you see," Thomas warned. "You will be afraid."

"Aren't you, uncle?"

"I am, Nathan, because I've seen the plague before. I tremble when I think of those sore-covered bodies."

A group of rough-looking men were packing a wagon in the street ahead of them. Suddenly three of the men blocked their way. "What are you doing here, Quakers?" Nathan drew back, his heart beating uncontrollably.

"We go to help the sick." Uncle Thomas's forceful tone surprised Nathan.

"You're going into that street?" a man who seemed to be the leader asked.

"Yes, let us pass, please."

The anger melted from the man's voice. "If you want to kill yourselves, at least leave the boy. We will see him home safely." Nathan's body stiffened. The claws of the rabbit's foot hurt as he pressed it deeply into his palm.

Thomas turned to Nathan. "If you come with us, your mother will be very unhappy. I leave the decision to you, Nathan. Search your heart, as you have learned in our meetings."

Actually, Nathan daydreamed at meetings. But the decision was not difficult. He would never go with men he did not know or trust. So he shook his head and drew closer to Thomas as he said, "I want to go with my uncle."

As they walked on, he heard one man warn, "Take care." Then the men mumbled about the crazy Quakers. *Maybe they were right!*

A slight wind from the river brought a smell Nathan recognized, overpowering the normal stench of the streets. He tried not to breathe, fighting a desire to clap his hand over his nose and mouth. His stomach churned. The smell of death made him light-headed and queasy. For a moment, he felt like bolting, running all the way home and slamming the door behind him. But he couldn't do that now. If he did, he would always think of himself as a coward. His uncle had faith in him, and he must be able to say he had searched for Henry Crispin.

A huge rat darted boldly across the deserted street. The creature stopped at the sight of the men, sniffed the air haughtily with waving whiskers, and then continued examining a pile of garbage. He stood on his two hind legs, almost walking like a man. Nathan had seen a duke dressed in black velvet who walked like that in his high-heeled, square-toed shoes.

The boy thought he was dreaming. Rats seemed to have replaced people. Only silence surrounded their tiny band, like a thick morning fog. Where were the hawkers hollering for people to buy their goods, the barking dogs, the yowling cats? The whole noisy rhythm of the streets had been waved away by some terrible sorcerer.

Trembling, Nathan turned in a circle as he walked.

"Everyone is gone—even the animals."

"The cats and dogs have been killed, no doubt," Isaac answered directly.

"Why?"

"It is believed they spread the plague," Thomas told him.

The men found an empty wagon and hitched up two wandering horses, to remove as many of the sick as possible.

As Nathan entered the first house, his feet would not budge beyond the front door. Stale onion, mingled with the horrid scent of two dead hens, filled the tightly closed room. A man's body lay on a rush mat. His throat bulged to twice its normal size, almost as if he had no neck. Even in the closed, dim room, the black spots on his face stood out like finger marks of the devil. Runny sores covered his bare legs.

"Not dead long—he's still warm, pour soul," Isaac commented as he covered him with a blanket from an upstairs bed.

Nathan tried to hold his breath. His stomach rolled and heaved. Isaac offered his red kerchief, and the boy took it gratefully. But he still had to leave the house. He steadied himself by holding on to a hitching post until the men came out.

"Are you all right?" Thomas asked.

Nathan nodded. "The smell! That man couldn't have been plucking chickens when he died!"

"No, the fowl is used to cure the plague . . . placed on the runny sores to draw out the poison. Those peeled onions—if left in the house ten days—are supposed to absorb infection, too," Uncle Thomas explained.

"Nothing works," Isaac added. "The physicians are helpless."

"Tie that kerchief around your face, Nathan," Thomas suggested. Then they assigned Nathan to hold the horses when they stopped at each house. Nathan soon learned that if there was no answer when the men knocked, those inside were beyond help. The men would come out silently and scratch an *X,* the sign of the plague, on the door.

Three houses were already painted with huge red *X*s, but the men entered anyway. Nathan did not know how they found the courage.

"Will we take the cart to the pesthouse?" Nathan asked. "That's where plague victims belong."

"Some to my home, and the rest to Saint Giles, the pesthouse," Isaac replied, tucking a blanket around a man already on the wagon.

"To your home? To have them die there?" Nathan could not understand. He would never want these sore-infested bodies near his family. "Why do you want to take care of them? They should all go to the pesthouse," he asserted.

"I know, Nathan, but so few survive there. Perhaps more will live at my home. These faces would haunt me forever if I didn't help them. My wife and I have no children, nor relatives. We have no place to go if we leave London. And if we leave our home, we may lose it."

A man on the cart motioned to Isaac. "Take me to your home, please," he whispered through his bluish black throat. "Don't take me to the pesthouse."

"I promise," Isaac replied, smoothing the man's hair away from his face.

Nathan watched the river lap at its slippery edge. Henry Crispin could have fallen in. Many had drowned in the Thames River. He might have been taken aboard a ship, pressed into service against his will. How he dreaded facing Matt and his family!

A shrill cry rose above the wash of the river and the low moaning of the sick on the cart. He stepped back from the wagon. "Do you hear that wailing?"

"A tabby cat," his uncle offered.

"I don't believe there's a cat in this area," Nathan protested. He and his uncle traced the wailing, while Isaac and Miles stayed with the cart. They turned into a filthy alley among houses that crowded down to the water.

With each step, the cry grew louder.

"It's coming from in here." Nathan knocked at a door, but the only sound was the continued screeching. His uncle swung the door open, banging it against the wall. Nathan stepped into the room cautiously.

His heart stopped, as he saw a woman who looked dead rocking back and forth in the middle of the room. Her bony hand clutched a cradle at her side. The wailing seemed to come from there.

"Let me examine her," Thomas told Nathan. "You may go outside, if you wish."

"No, I'll stay," the boy answered weakly, although his knees shook and his feet barely moved toward the gaunt figure. Nathan gasped as her eyes turned toward them, and her swollen blue lips parted, trying to form words.

# 4

NATHAN AND HIS UNCLE leaned closer to hear the hoarse whisper issuing from the woman's swollen throat.

"I've stayed alive in case someone would come," she rasped. "I've prayed and prayed. . . ." She stopped speaking, gulping for breath with a wheeze that made Nathan's throat tighten.

Thomas offered her water, but she refused to swallow. Or the pain of trying was too great.

"Save my baby," she continued between gasps.

"We will help you," Thomas promised. "Can you tell us where your relatives live?"

The woman rolled her head weakly from side to side. "I have none. Don't bother to search." The red stain in her eyes almost hid the enlarged pupils that stared at Nathan's uncle. "My husband is dead . . . there is no one else. Take her . . . please."

Her voice rose with the urgency of her desire.

As she spoke, Nathan leaned over the cradle. The red-faced baby stopped crying, startled, he thought, to see an unfamiliar face—or any face at all, since she had screamed at the ceiling for so long. Tears poured from the sides of her eyes, flowing into a crust that had formed from all her crying. She reached out to him.

Intense pity forced him to lift the child and comfort her.

"My baby . . ." The mother's body shook. "Take my Bridget. Help her. Please swear you will care for her."

"Can you see us?" Thomas asked. "We're Friends . . . Quakers."

"I don't care. . . . If she lives, I hope she will have half your strength. . . ."

*Uncle Thomas is strong,* Nathan realized. *But with a different kind of strength than a soldier . . . a different kind of courage. . . .*

The baby snatched the flask Nathan offered her and gulped the water greedily, spilling it down her chin.

Because of the baby's silence, her mother's low voice now filled the room. "I will pray for you all." Her lips closed.

His uncle covered the silent form with a blanket. Nathan feared he might break down sobbing, but the baby needed him. He was glad he had decided to stay and help the men.

"We must find a new place for you, little Bridget," Uncle Thomas said as he searched the room, finally locating the baby's clothing in a heavy wooden chest. He took her from Nathan and tried to remove her wet dress and slip on a dry one.

"I can dress her, uncle." Nathan had often helped with his little brother. As he dressed the child, he found a tiny golden cross on a chain around her neck.

"These people couldn't afford a jeweled cross," Uncle Thomas said as he turned the cross, removing his spectacles to squint at the jeweler's initials on the back. "Perhaps it is a family heirloom," he suggested.

"Or a christening gift."

"That's possible. Wealthy relatives must have given her this richly trimmed cradle, too." Uncle Thomas observed.

Nathan's foot hit something hard under the cradle. Leaning down, he spied a gleaming object, which turned out to be a silver flask, decorated with a unicorn and lion that held the royal coat of arms.

Uncle Thomas took the flask, removing the top to sniff its contents. He frowned. "I believe it's angelica root mixed with powdered unicorn's horn—another well-known cure for the plague."

"Another cure that doesn't work," Nathan said sarcastically. "This flask must be very valuable. Shall we keep it for the baby?" His uncle's brow knotted as he stared. at the silver bottle.

"No, it's best we don't. Everything—bedding, clothes—must be thrown into the river."

"They carry the plague?" Nathan asked.

"We don't know. It spreads through families and streets somehow. No one knows. A favored few survive. To be safe, we won't take anything but what the child is wearing now."

Nathan eyed the beautiful flask, knowing how valuable it must be. "Uncle Thomas, where do apothecaries find unicorn's horn? The creature doesn't live in England."

"Nor in the known world, Nathan. But the horn of the ancient unicorn is said to have great power, because of the Old Testament. I don't know what apothecaries use now. I'm certain that whoever buys powdered unicorn's horn is being cheated a little."

Outside the house, Nathan, holding the baby, watched as his uncle scratched a grisly *X* on the door with his knife. Isaac and Miles would come tomorrow with other Friends and bury the bodies in the limepits outside the city. The thought made Nathan shiver.

"How did the plague end before?" Nathan asked.

"Some say the fire purged the air," Uncle Thomas began. "Others say the plague was dying before the fire began."

As they walked toward the wagon, Nathan felt a nudge at the back of his thigh. In the corner of his eye, he saw the light brown fur of a stray dog. The animal whimpered, and Nathan stopped to pet it.

"Leave him be, Nathan," his uncle warned. "A babe is enough for your mother today. Remember, the animal might carry the plague."

"But we might have it, too." A shudder forced Nathan to pause. He thought of the dog's cruel future. His owner—if he had one—was probably dead. The stray would be killed by whoever had destroyed the other animals. Nathan's hand slipped into his jacket and drew out the now crumbled slice of cheese the shopkeeper had given him. Carefully he dropped it so his uncle would not notice.

Bridget had been inside so long she barely opened her swollen eyes. Nathan saw deep brown through her puffy, red lids. She squirmed in all directions in his arms, giving Nathan hope that she was not sick. Isaac and Miles agreed that the babe seemed well now. But from their glances, he knew they felt the child was doomed. Nathan remembered Edmund as a fat, rosy baby, whereas Bridget's arms were thin and chalk white. Those swollen, red eyelids dominated her narrow, pale face.

"Mother will know what to do for her," he told everyone confidently. His feet dragged now. He felt as though someone had tied two great stones to them as he forced himself, one step at a time, to walk beside the wagon.

The chilling toll of the death bell hung in the air long after it had stopped ringing. Nathan was thankful that sorrowful bell would never ring for him; Quakers did not allow it.

On normal days, drivers of carts, coaches, and drays argued when they could not pass each other on the narrow streets. The driver who shouted the loudest won—a scene that provided grand entertainment for the children on the street. But today, people flattened themselves against the bricks when they saw the cart and its passengers.

Nathan marveled at the sudden absence of shouting hawkers as the baby's head dropped on his shoulder. The exhausted child slept, and her tiny weight grew heavier with each step. Just when he knew he would have to rest, they arrived at his uncle's door. Isaac and Miles tied the horses to an iron post.

"Come in and rest, Friends." Thomas opened the door.

In the parlor, blanket rolls covered the floor. The Crispin family had arrived. Mother and Jennett were serving boiled mutton and cabbage for supper, so the weary men joined them.

But Nathan could not wait for mother to examine the baby. "Please look at her, mother. She's so thin." On the farm, his mother had been their physician and apothecary. She often consulted a worn book of cures given to her by her mother—and passed down by her grandmother

41

and, before that, her great-grandmother.

"She still seems well, only hungry—starved, poor babe." Mother curiously examined the delicate golden cross. "Bridget must be about six to nine months old, though she's tiny." All the girls gathered around the baby.

"We'll feed her a cup of warm broth." Mother dipped a cup into the large black pot, waited until the liquid cooled, and then skimmed off the fat.

"May I feed her?" Jennett asked.

"Let her drink slowly, Jennett," mother cautioned. "In an hour, we will feed her again."

When Bridget was finished, Jennett rocked her. "Will she be our baby?" she asked, playing with the youngster's tiny fist. Mother and Uncle Thomas exchanged worried glances. Nathan knew the last thing they needed was another child to care for. They tried to hide their situation from the children, but Nathan knew trouble approached from all directions—the authorities, the plague. How long could they shield themselves from the descending danger? He vividly remembered Miles's slip about arrests.

"If the baby goes to a home, she will surely die." Nathan's mother referred to the few orphanages for unwanted children.

"I'll care for her, mother." Jennett cradled Bridget in her arms.

"I feel responsible, Ellen." Thomas sank wearily into a chair. "The mother gave her to us, because there were no relatives. Her death wish was that the child be properly cared for."

The Crispin girls and Jennett played with Bridget while Edmund sat frowning in the far corner of the room.

Suddenly he shouted, "We don't need a baby!" and stalked upstairs. Nathan followed as his little brother complained loudly. The older boy tried to explain about orphanages, but Edmund refused to understand.

"Nathan, Edmund," Uncle Thomas called. "Isaac and Miles are leaving."

Isaac's two large hands engulfed Nathan's. "You did a man's work today. May God be with you and your family."

"And with you, Isaac." Nathan turned to the other man. "And you, too, Miles."

"Isaac," mother called as she handed him a sack, "this cabbage is for you."

"No, Ellen. You will need the food."

"Take it, please." She held it out. "You will need broth for the sick. Food will soon be difficult to find in the city."

Nathan knew they did not have much food themselves, especially now that the Crispin family and the orphaned baby were with them. Why should mother give their precious food to people who would probably die anyway? Then he looked at Bridget. He did not want her to die.

"We will watch your house, Thomas," Isaac

promised as they left. "And the Crispin's."

The children clustered around the doorway to watch them lead the wagon away.

"May I play outside?" Edmund asked, jumping onto the cobblestones. Nathan shook his head, pulling his little brother up the step and back into the house. He bolted the door without even asking his uncle. Edmund squirmed away and ran crying to his mother. "Nate won't let me play outside!"

"Hush, Edmund," came the quiet answer.

Everyone except Edmund seemed unwilling to talk. Nathan never imagined eleven people could be so silent, even Quakers.

Finally, Edmund gave up complaining and stared glumly out the front window. The air seemed alive with fear no one wanted to voice as the death bell tolled again.

Nathan was alarmed by the dazed look in Mrs. Crispin's eyes. When she tried to speak, her voice broke and tears appeared in her eyes. Finally, Uncle Thomas spoke to her gently about resting, and Matt helped her upstairs to the good bed. Mary and Priscilla stayed there with her.

*My own mother seems stronger now,* Nathan thought gratefully as he and Matt helped Uncle Thomas settle the other children into blanket rolls on the floor.

"When will papa come?" little Abigail Crispin asked.

"I don't know," Matt replied as he tucked a blanket around her chin. "Say prayers for him, Abigail." She nodded solemnly, her light brown hair glinting in the candlelight.

The candle's flames bent gently with the drafts, decorating the semi-darkness with lacy shadows. When Uncle Thomas snuffed the flames, swift gray swirls of smoke fell toward the floor, filling Nathan's lungs with the warm smell of melting wax.

Though exhaustion penetrated every corner of his body, Nathan was kept awake by the other children's breathing. But none of the ordinary sounds came to his ears, except the whimpering of a dog and the rumble of passing coaches. Even the night watchman had deserted his post. His "All's well" never came.

# 5

PINPOINTS OF LIGHT pierced the numbness of Nathan's mind. Then the lights joined together to form the flame of a candle. Nathan opened his eyes to focus on the flame and the man who held it.

"Time to rise, Nathan," Uncle Thomas said.

*No!* His body needed hours more sleep; it must be the middle of the night. He turned slightly, moaning in protest.

Soon he forced his body to move, helping Uncle Thomas and Matt tie each bedroll securely. His mother gave Bridget some more broth, and the children some leftover rabbit pie, mutton, and cabbage. There was enough for seconds, but after that the kettle was empty, as black inside as out.

After this unusually large breakfast, they gathered around Uncle Thomas. He carefully matched the burdens to the size of each child, dividing their food and slipping it into the bedrolls. Abigail and Edmund carried the smallest. Still,

*"I can carry more, uncle!"* Edmund boasted.

Edmund's roll reached to the top of his reddish blond hair.

"I can carry more!" he boasted.

Uncle Thomas lifted the boy's roll. "This will grow heavy in time, Edmund." Nathan and Matt took two of the larger packs and Uncle Thomas, the biggest, along with his books strapped into a bundle. Nathan should have realized his uncle would never leave his most precious treasure, even for a day or two. Still, the extra weight made a heavy burden for the small man.

"I'll carry Bridget," Jennett offered.

Mary and Priscilla brought their mother downstairs. She did what Nathan's mother asked her, but refused any food.

At the last minute, his mother ran upstairs to see if there was anything else she should take. She returned with Edmund's old corals and some of his baby clothes.

"Bridget can teeth on these ocean corals. They will protect her from witches' spells, too," she said as she slipped them over the baby's head.

As they stepped outside, they met an unexpected visitor—the dog Nathan had fed the day before. The stray jumped all over him, barking a happy greeting.

Uncle Thomas frowned at Nathan, who shrugged his shoulders. The boy could not help smiling at the friendly animal. As Edmund petted the dog, Nathan explained what had happened.

"Don't encourage him to follow us," Uncle Thomas warned.

But "Dog," as Edmund called him, needed no encouragement to trot briskly at their heels. He even brought his own food—a huge bone from a joint of beef picked out of the garbage. Often the dog stopped to gnaw on his prize. But as soon as they moved a short distance away, he grabbed his bone and caught up with them.

The pewter fog swirled around three street urchins still sleeping huddled together in a dirty alley. The boy wondered if their homeless fate might hit his family, and the chilly thought hung in his mind like the mist that was clinging to his coat.

Edmund, delighted to be out-of-doors, ran ahead of them for a while. When he finally tired, the little boy dropped back, walking beside Nathan and Matt, chattering with continual questions about yesterday. Nathan answered each one as kindly as possible, telling how they found Bridget and about her beautiful cradle and golden cross. He described the silver flask etched with the unicorn and the lion that bore the royal coat of arms.

"I wish I could have seen it. What's a unicorn?" Edmund stopped to pick up a pebble and examined it closely.

Nathan described the prancing, one-horned beast.

"Where can I see one? We saw the lions at the

Tower." Edmund tossed the small rock into the damp fog.

"Uncle Thomas said they lived once in a far-off land. But England has none to see."

"Then how do we know about them?" Edmund persisted.

Nathan was about to tell his little brother to be quiet, when the little boy groaned, "My feet hurt."

"We've barely started," Nathan reminded him.

"When we're out of London, we'll rest," promised Uncle Thomas as they walked through the poor hovels on the outskirts of the city.

Now Nathan's wish had come true. They were near the country. A few others seemed to be leaving the city, too, but most must have left yesterday.

He noticed Jennett falling behind. *She's tiring,* he thought, as he joined her.

"Let me take Bridget for a while, Jennett." His sister smiled and gave him the carefully bundled baby.

Only her dark eyes showed from a tiny opening in the folds of the damp gray blanket. They were not as swollen as yesterday and seemed curious and lively. She had eaten greedily this morning, and they all hoped she would survive. *Why do some die and others stay well?* Nathan puzzled.

His burden grew heavier as Uncle Thomas led them south of the city. Nathan watched Matt's mother, who only spoke when asked a direct question. Mostly, she stared off in the distance at some imaginary ghost. Even when Matt and his sisters tried to hold her hands or cheer her, she ignored them.

At last, rays of sun forced their way through the glum morning. *The warmth will brighten us,* Nathan thought. But soon sweat gathered under his hat and gradually ran down the sides of his face.

Finally Uncle Thomas halted them. "Let's rest, children." Nathan dropped his blanket roll immediately and sank down with the baby. He threw his hat to the ground and wiped his hair and forehead with his red kerchief.

"I'm hungry," Edmund said as he pulled a long green weed from the ground and nibbled at the end.

All the children watched anxiously as Uncle Thomas sliced a loaf of bread. What Nathan wanted was a trencher piled high with meat and cheese. He swallowed hard and forced himself to eat the bread slowly.

"Take small bites," Nathan cautioned Edmund. He had not expected his uncle to slice cheese for them. But the small piece eased his hunger. Then they each drank a sip from a leather flask.

"When can we go home?" Edmund whimpered.

Nathan drew his brother to him. "Why don't we pretend we're on an adventure?" Little Edmund's eyes lit up.

"We'll pretend we're searching an island for buried treasure," Nathan suggested as Jennett put tiny bits of cheese in Bridget's mouth.

"Pirates? Like Morgan?" Edmund's blue eyes widened, sparkling.

"Yes," Nathan nodded. "While we're walking, we'll look for signs of pirates. And where they buried their treasure."

"And lions, like the ones at the Tower," Edmund exclaimed, "and unicorns!"

When Uncle Thomas rose, Edmund picked up his blanket roll eagerly. Nathan saw that his uncle meant to carry the baby, plus his already large burden.

"Let me carry your books then, uncle," he offered. But as they started on, he felt as if someone had added rocks to his own pack. He wondered how long he could walk through the grassy fields with the added weight of his uncle's books.

Still, he played the pirate game with Edmund, exclaiming whenever his little brother spotted a broken twig or a footprint. "The pirates have been here!" Edmund would shout. "Their treasure is hidden this way!"

They stopped to rest twice, and each time their uncle gave them a sip from the flask. What remained in the leather bottle would not last until morning. The more Nathan thought about his aching throat, the worse his thirst became.

"I hear water!" Matt cried. Nathan heard the

stream rushing somewhere in the grass ahead of them, and both boys raced for it. He did not care whether the water was good or bad. He plunged his face into the clear brook and drank until he heard his stomach sloshing. The other children followed. He and Matt came up laughing, water dripping down their necks and clothes. Dog jumped in, swimming like an otter. When he pulled himself from the water, he shook his sopping body, splattering all of them.

Red-faced Uncle Thomas wiped the sweat from his forehead and drank, too. "This looks like a good spot to spend the night." The tall grass would hide them, and they could sleep warmly between some fallen logs by the creek bed.

Apples, cold beef, and cheese made their dinner, and then they settled under the blankets for the evening. Edmund huddled close to Nathan, whispering, "Aren't you afraid?"

Nathan nodded. He had to be honest.

"The night air is bad for the children," Nathan's mother warned Thomas.

"Leave your hats and bonnets on," he advised them, "and pull your blankets up as high as possible."

Nathan loved the smell of the cool night air. He deliberately breathed deeply, for he knew they would sleep in a stuffy room with drawn bed curtains when they reached a town. At last, his little brother fell asleep.

Nathan rubbed his sore ankle. Now that he had a free moment, he realized it still hurt. His toes felt hot and swollen. He dozed off, but woke often, not used to the noises of the night creatures.

A branch crackled, and Nathan sat up, straining his ears to hear more. Dog growled low in his throat.

*Wake up. Stay on guard,* his instincts told him.

Silently, he counted the members of their tiny band to see if someone might be off in the darkness. *Ten forms, and the small bundle resting by Jennett made eleven.*

The uneasy boy squinted into the dawning morning. *Yes!* He saw movement rustling in the grass!

Dog stood up, barking sharply.

"Who are you?" he demanded. "What do you want?" He tried to speak deeply and gruffly, but his voice chose to crack, as it often did.

A rough voice pierced the shadows. "Do you have any food?"

# 6

THE STARTLED CHILDREN, Uncle Thomas, and the two women sat up in the dim light as Dog barked fiercely. Mother tried to quiet the little ones.

"Do you have any food?" the unfriendly voice asked again.

"Do *you* have any food?" Uncle Thomas answered.

Nathan felt the ground under his blanket until he found a rock that could be used as a weapon. They had to protect themselves. He pressed another rock into Matt's hand. At first, the other boy did not take hold of it. But then, he tapped on the top of Nathan's fingers to signal that he understood.

"Yes, we have food," came the gruff answer. "But we can always use more!" Nathan's grip on the rock tightened.

The "we" so alarmed him that his heart began to

pound, until he could hear almost nothing else. He peered through the dusk to see at least two shadowy forms that were growing larger. His arm went rigid as he clutched the rock.

"How many are you?" a man called through the dimness.

"Mama!" Edmund cried out, stirring from his sleep. "Mama! I'm hungry!" The younger girls whimpered, and Bridget joined in.

Nathan heard murmuring through the tall grass.

Uncle Thomas spoke up. "We had to leave the London riverfront in a hurry. Can you give us extra food?" The baby cried with the full force of her lungs now.

"Hungry children!" the disgusted voice spat out the words. "You bring the plague with you!" Nathan heard scuffling feet run off. He hugged Edmund for his well-timed complaint.

His uncle's quick-wittedness had saved them all.

"I'm hungry!" Edmund repeated.

They rose to eat cheese and the last slices of bread. Nathan swallowed all the water his insides would hold.

"We'd best leave." Uncle Thomas rolled up his blanket—this time with his books inside—and tied the large parcel together with rope.

"We might catch fish and rabbits here," Matt offered.

"Like the stream by our farm in Yorkshire," Edmund added.

"Yes, but we cannot light a fire to cook them, boys. Someone might be drawn by the smoke. Many are fleeing London now who will be hungry. And hungry people aren't particular about who has been near the plague and who hasn't. They want food."

"Uncle Thomas, where are we going?" Nathan could not wait any longer to know the end of their journey.

"If I cannot find a safe home for you in the country, I have friends in Deal and enough money to pay your passage to Holland."

"There are groups of Friends in Holland who will welcome us," mother explained.

"My father," Matt burst in. "I want to look for my father!" Nathan put his arm around his friend's shoulder. "I know how you feel, Matt, but we must stay together."

"When we are in Deal, I will write and try to locate your father," Uncle Thomas promised the boy.

*He thinks letters will solve everything.* Nathan swung his blanket roll to his shoulder. He knew they would never see Henry Crispin again. . . .

Matt's mother buried her face in her hands, sobbing softly. Matt put his arms around her as her daughters clutched her skirts.

"We must leave," Uncle Thomas spoke sternly.

He handed each child his pack. "We aren't safe here any longer."

Matt lifted his own bedroll and his mother's, too. But she took it from him. "I'll be all right, Matthew. If only I knew what happened." The tightness inside Nathan relaxed as he realized she understood what was happening around her.

He watched curiously as his uncle ripped a red kerchief into shreds and knotted the strips together. Then he tied one end around Dog's neck and fastened the other to a tree by the stream.

"Uncle!" Nathan protested. "You can't tie him up! He helped us. He warned us when those men came."

"I know, Nathan, but we can't feed him for long. And there is the chance that he will bark and give us away."

"We can't leave him tied here." The other children joined Nathan in his protest.

"He will soon pull away from this flimsy tie. But that should give us enough time to get away." Uncle Thomas gathered the bones left over from supper and piled them by Dog, who wagged his tail.

Then they left.

Nathan wanted to turn back and release Dog. The animal tried to follow them, pulling to the end of the tie. But his head jerked back, and then he yipped and whimpered. As they moved further away, he began to bark.

Soon the barking grew fainter and fainter, until they no longer heard it. The memory of the helpless dog, jerking his head back on the tie, made their flight more sorrowful. But Nathan knew Dog must be a superb tracker. Hadn't he followed them through the streets of London—streets that reeked with a thousand smells to drive him off the scent? Or maybe he had simply kept them in sight. . . . Nathan looked back, hoping to see Dog bounding toward them.

He always walked last to make certain none of the younger ones fell behind. Walking through these rough fields, pebbles jabbed through his leather soles, and often he stumbled on the uneven ground. At noonday, they dropped to the dirt too tired to speak. Even Uncle Thomas seemed to have run out of words. Silently, mother handed each child an apple.

Nathan rested the back of his head on his blanket and gazed at the cloud pictures forming in the sky. *This is better than being trapped in a small house in London,* he told himself. *Even if we did leave Dog behind.* Slowly, a vibration broke his thoughts. He turned his body and listened to the ground. Hoofbeats rumbled the turf beneath him. Horses, approaching from the east! His mouth opened to shout, but Uncle Thomas warned, "Quiet, children! Don't say a word. Keep down in the grass!"

Nathan buried his face in the dust, not daring to

breathe. With one hand, he held his brother down and ordered, "Silence, Edmund. Don't even ask why."

The hoofbeats slowed. Now the horses were very close, so close that Nathan smelled the sweating horsehair and heard the clank of metal. The riders wore swords! He closed his eyes and prayed they would go away.

Little Edmund's body trembled under Nathan's arm, but not a sound slipped from his brother's tightly closed lips. Only when Nathan heard the horses turn away did he gasp in a dusty breath.

But at that moment, Bridget squealed for attention. Too late, Jennett clapped her hand over the baby's mouth. Above them loomed the horses and their riders, casting shadows like an eclipse of the sun.

"Look what's hiding here—Quakers!" A mounted soldier parted the grass with his sword.

"Quakers!" The other soldier spat out the word, as though he had discovered thieves. They sheated their swords. "Why are you hiding here?"

Slowly, Nathan stood up, holding his shaking brother. Uncle Thomas mumbled something, but the soldier interrupted.

"You are disloyal to the king!"

Edmund ran to cling to his mother's waist.

"Dissenter!" The other soldier shouted as he dismounted. "You will come with us—all of you! We will find out what you're up to."

Nathan stared at the men, not believing his ears. What had they done?

"Take me," Uncle Thomas offered. "Leave the women and children. We only left London because of the plague." His lids closed slowly over his gray-blue eyes and then popped open again, as though he hoped the soldiers would vanish by this simple method.

Nathan wanted to follow his uncle's example and offer himself rather than the others, but fear silenced him. He felt like his body had turned to a statue with eyes.

"This boy," the soldier said roughly, pushing Nathan's shoulder, "is practically as big as you, and this one, too." He yanked Matt by the arm. "You are all coming with us," he announced as he mounted his horse.

"Line up there, with your two wives, Quaker!" Both soldiers roared with laughter. A flash exploded in Nathan's brain. Quickly, he pulled at the nearest soldier's leg. But the other soldier struck Nathan on the ear with the back of his hand. The boy reeled and crumpled in the grass. His breath deserted him with a *whump* when he hit the ground unable to even cry out. His teeth dug into his lip. Warm blood, mixed with dirt, filled his mouth as his uncle and Matt helped him up.

Jennett tried to calm the Crispin girls.

"Move!" the soldier ordered.

He pressed his red kerchief hard on his bleeding mouth. *I'll run,* he thought. *If I zigzag across the field, the soldiers might not be able to find me, even with their big horses.* They should have scattered when they first heard the noise. Then, at least some of them would have gotten away. Uncle Thomas did not think of that. *Everything he has done has led us to this, even to tying up Dog, who might have warned us.*

Nathan walked until he felt he could move no longer. The soldiers allowed them to drink and rest at the stream where they had spent the night. Nathan saw them staring at Jennett and Mary.

"How old are you?" one of them asked his sister.

Shaking, Jennett barely answered. "Ten." Mary took her hand protectively.

"And you?" the other soldier asked Mary. The girl drew herself up and with surprising pride and a calm, defiant look said, "Eleven."

The two soldiers exchanged glances.

Nathan shook with anger. Matt understood, but he whispered that the men were only talking. The side of Nathan's head where he had been struck throbbed. His eyes blurred, and, when they resumed their walk, he stumbled often. The pain he felt in his head and foot almost numbed his fear of their destination.

If someone placed a sword in his hands, he knew he would try to kill those soldiers, even though violence was against their faith. But not Uncle

Thomas. He would not fight, even if it meant his own death. Nathan did not want to suffer and die silently with the other Quakers. He would not let anything happen to any of them without a battle. Wasn't King Henry V a mighty fighter as a boy? Warriors ruled the world. They had all the power.

Nathan felt his strength deserting him as they marched wearily into the town. Unfriendly eyes bored into him, so he stared at the smooth gray cobblestones beneath his feet. All the time, he hoped none of this was real, that he would wake in the curtained bed at his uncle's house. But then they reached the dark, massive door of a stone prison.

One soldier dismounted and pulled an iron ring that opened the wooden door. Nathan did not want to walk the last steps and enter—nor did any of them. But the other soldier dismounted and pushed each hesitant captive through the doorway. Then day became night. The prison wall closed behind them, and Nathan felt as he had when the mud splattered against his back.

"Why are we here?" Edmund cried.

The Crispin girls trembled and clung together.

"I don't like it. . . . I want to go home!" Edmund wailed.

No one spoke to him. But Mother pulled the little boy close, and he hid his head in her skirt.

"Hal!" one of their captors shouted.

Heavy-soled boots echoed from a dark stairway

that led underground. A man with a huge ring on his belt stepped into view, wiping food from his shaggy gray beard with his sleeve. He tossed a small meat bone to a corner of the room and rolled his tongue over his upper lip.

"Hurry up, man! We want a cell for these Quakers."

Though Nathan heard the words, he could not believe them.

Thomas protested, "We must see a magistrate. We cannot be imprisoned until we come before a judge."

"Quiet!" the soldier shouted. "We deal with nonconformists our way. You and your traitor's plots!"

"We must be brought before a magistrate. You cannot do this!" Uncle Thomas persisted with a stubbornness that astonished Nathan.

"We'll do what we want."

"Keep quiet," Hal, the old jailor, broke in, trying to warn Nathan's uncle.

"You are breaking the law. We have done nothing." Thomas answered again.

Without any warning, the taller soldier struck Thomas across the face, throwing the small man to the floor. Nathan froze as the soldier started to strike him again. But Jennett dashed from between the crying children and threw herself over her uncle's body, screaming, "Stop!"

Her blue eyes flared, and then closed tightly as she ducked her head to take the next blow. But the startled soldier lowered his hand and leered at the girl. After a few seconds, Jennett opened her eyes, realizing she would not be hit. She helped her uncle to his feet.

"Anything for you, little lady," the soldier nodded, winking at Hal and their other captor. "Lock them up."

A reddish knot stood out on Uncle Thomas's forehead, and he seemed dazed. Nathan noticed his spectacles lying on the floor.

"Come along, all of ye." The bent old Hal motioned for them to follow.

Nathan lagged behind to scoop up the spectacles. One of the soldiers jabbed him roughly in the ribs. "Move!" the man ordered. The boy watched Jennett tenderly leading the unsteady Uncle Thomas. When they had needed help, she was the one who had been brave enough, and quick enough, to act. Nathan was ashamed it had not been he.

"Don't bring any more in here, captain," old Hal grumbled. "Half the countryside's in jail already, and we only have three cells left."

"Just do your job, old man," the soldier snapped, "and we'll do ours."

Then the soldiers pushed them to the top of a stone stairwell that led underneath the main floor. Foul, damp air struck Nathan's nostrils, making him gasp. He peered into the darkness but only saw the first four steps.

*Not me! This can't be real.* He forced down the scream that rose in his throat. As the cold of the first step pierced his worn leather soles, a chill traveled deep into his leg bones. He could not control the shiver that engulfed him.

# 7

"I WON'T GO DOWN THERE!" Edmund balked at the top of the stairs.

"Walk or you'll fly down," the soldier commanded.

Nathan lifted his brother by the waist, clutching the blanket roll and his uncle's spectacles in his other hand. This extra burden made his footing down the slippery, worn steps even more unsure. A thousand feet must have tread the stones before him, wearing treacherous grooves in the stairs. He forced his numb hand to hold the blanket roll, because he knew how fortunate they were that their possessions had not been taken. Abigail and Priscilla clung to Matt's arms. Mary Crispin helped her mother, and Nathan's mother carried the baby. His arms prickled as the moist, dark air of the underground hole touched his face. Edmund gripped his neck so tightly Nathan could barely breathe.

But shallow breathing was a blessing in this musty stench. With every gasp, he fought to keep himself from becoming sick. As his eyes grew accustomed to the dim corridor, he saw the still forms of human beings slumped in the straw-filled cells they passed.

Abruptly the cell openings changed from barred frames to doors, and the soldiers halted them. Nathan pictured the door to his own tomb.

"All right," the old man ordered. "Half of ye in this one."

"Matthew," Thomas asked, "can you manage your family?" Matt nodded, his lips trembling, and stepped into the shadowy hole with his two sisters clinging to his arms. Mary led her mother in. The woman had not spoken a word since their capture. She just stared straight ahead as though her mind were elsewhere. *A blessed escape*, Nathan thought.

"Go thou with God." Thomas's choked voice echoed in the stone corridor as Hal turned the key in the rusty lock.

"And with you." He heard Matt's muffled answer as the door closed on its rusty hinges.

Hal and the soldiers snickered. "God doesn't know this place!"

These were the first words Nathan agreed with all day.

"Here's yer cell—right next to yer friends." Hal opened the door and motioned for them to enter.

Thomas protested weakly, "I would like to speak to someone in authority...." But one of the soldiers interrupted by shoving him into the cell.

"Everyone in here wants to speak to someone," the old jail-keeper answered. "The king wants ye here, safe from yer troublemakin'. No one cares what happens to ye. The further out of sight, the better. Learn that, and make the best of it."

The heavy door swung shut with such a clank that Nathan dropped his blanket roll and collapsed into the dank straw with Edmund. Hal's key ring jingled, becoming softer and softer as the old man and the soldiers returned above.

Silence filled the cell. What could be said? . . . At last, Bridget squealed.

"Be quiet!" Edmund cried. "I hate that baby!"

"Sssh, Edmund," his mother said, hugging him. In the dim light, her features seemed to be chisled in gray stone.

"That baby gave us away. It's her fault!" the boy protested.

"She's only a baby," Jennett argued.

"We would have been caught anyway, Edmund," Uncle Thomas added. "Those soldiers were searching the whole area. They would have caught us eventually. . . . Ellen, I'm so sorry." He rested his elbows on his knees and held his forehead in his hands.

"This isn't your fault, Thomas." She touched his face tenderly, feeling the knot that continued to rise in the middle of his forehead.

"I tried to make the best decision at every point. But we've ended up here," Thomas said.

"Uncle Thomas," Nathan volunteered and held out his hand. "I picked up your spectacles."

"Oh." His uncle sat upright. "I'd forgotten them. Thank you, Nathan." He examined the dirty glass carefully. A tiny crack marred one corner of the right lens. "I'm fortunate they weren't completely smashed." He slipped the wires over his ears. "How could I read or write?" Nathan could not believe that his uncle still thought of reading and writing.

The man stood up slowly, steadying himself against the stone wall. Using one hand to keep from reeling, he examined their cell. Dust swirled about a thin beam of light from one small, barred window about eight feet above the floor. Irregular stones jutted out from the wall, so climbing to the opening was easy. Thomas climbed up slowly, clinging to the bars when he reached the top, and looked out. "An alley behind the prison. . . ." He climbed down. "The window is about half-an-arm's length above the street."

Nathan scrambled up the rocks to look at the alley and the sheer prison wall rising above them.

Edmund begged to see also, and Nathan jumped down to help him. His brother clutched the iron

*Nathan scrambled up the rocks to look at the alley and the sheer prison wall above them.*

bars, trying to push his face between them. Nathan realized that even if he could remove the bars somehow, the opening was only six inches high, too small for Edmund to slip through. And where would Edmund go if he did get out? Escape seemed impossible, but Nathan swore he would not remain in prison.

Edmund began to yell. "Hello. Hello there. Hello!" They all turned to look at the little boy clinging to the bars.

To Nathan's surprise, a voice answered him.

"Hello yourself, lad." The shadow of a man's boots cut off the light. Then, the boots disappeared abruptly, allowing the beam to pierce the shadowy cell once more.

"Don't go away!" Edmund pleaded.

"I must. . . ." The voice faded.

"Edmund, get down, please," mother cautioned.

The little boy refused to budge, forcing his face further through the bars.

"Hello! Here I am again!" the bright voice called.

The shadow of his boots again blocked the sun. "I can't stay. I must walk to the end of the prison and back."

"Why do you walk back and forth?" Edmund asked.

"Because I guard this alley, lad." The boots left, but Edmund clung to his perch. He waited until the man approached once more and called, "What's your name?"

"Christopher. . . . Christopher. . . ." The young voice trailed off.

"My name's Edmund Cowell!"

"Edmund," Thomas warned. "You must not cry out."

The little boy looked down. "All right, uncle. I'll whisper when he comes again."

After a few moments, Edmund loudly whispered, "Christopher, are you a soldier?"

"Aye, Christopher, the great hero—guard of the prison alley. That's me!"

The baby's cry stopped the conversation. She had stuffed straw in her mouth and was beginning to choke on it. Jennett removed the pieces, one by one, and put the coral on her gums, trying to teach her to suck on that.

Uncle Thomas and mother whispered together before allowing the children to eat. Bridget fussed loudly when she saw food withdrawn from the blanket roll. Edmund would not move from his perch. He almost lost his balance, though, when Christopher's face appeared at the bars.

*He couldn't be much older than I am!* Nathan realized.

"Hello, Edmund." Christopher's red hair turned the light beam rosy as he asked, "You have a babe in there, too?"

"Yes." Edmund spat out the word sourly.

They heard a sigh as Christopher's face vanished. "Christopher the great!" rang through the air. "Conqueror of the alley! Guard of dangerous mothers, children, and babes!"

"Christopher doesn't seem happy with his lot," Thomas mused.

"Edmund, ask how old he is," Nathan handed his younger brother a small piece of cheese. He noticed that his mother took a slice as large as the ones given to each of the children. But then she divided it with her brother.

"Christopher, how old are you?" Edmund asked between swallows.

"Fifteen years old" came the booming answer. "How old are you, Edmund?"

"Five."

*Fifteen years old and a soldier. He's only three years older than I,* Nathan thought, *and I'll soon be thirteen.*

"I had a sister who would have been five," Christopher commented. "She died of pox—my baby brother, too. . . ."

Edmund waited patiently for Christopher to march by again. "Why are you a soldier?" he asked.

"You never run out of questions, do you, Edmund?"

"No," Edmund answered matter-of-factly.

"My father's dead. My mom is sick. Work isn't easy to find, and we must have bread. . . . I did think I'd do more than guard an alley and babies. I had hoped for great adventure."

"I'm not a baby." Edmund said disgustedly as he finally hopped down from his perch. "Nathan, I don't want Christopher to guard me. I want to go home or have an adventure searching for pirates' treasure. When will they let us go?"

Nathan shook his head hopelessly.

When night came, Christopher told them he would leave.

"Who comes at night?" Edmund asked.

"No one."

*No guard at night!* Nathan knew that might be important to him. He had to escape from this tomb. . . . Swiftly, he drew his meat knife from the blanket roll. The guards had not taken anything. But he did not trust them and wanted to at least keep his knife. While the others curled into their blankets, he felt along the wall between the rocks.

At last—almost directly under the barred window—his fingers plunged deep into a crevice hidden below a jutting rock. *Had another prisoner tried to dig his way out?* The place swirled with ghosts. He slid the knife into this crevice as far as possible. Then a movement under his hand startled him. A bug ran up his arm. *Probably a large cockroach,* he thought. In the filtered moonlight, he saw only shadows. Quickly, he brushed it off and hit the creature with the hilt of his knife. His own fury shocked him.

The hole contained an unlucky nest of them, and Nathan could not stop until he destroyed every one of the slithering insects. No one woke, but his family turned restlessly in their sleep. Uncle Thomas groaned as he twisted from side to side.

Why had his uncle argued so stubbornly with the guards? "No doubt our fate would have been the same if we had come before the local magistrate," Nathan muttered to himself. "The king rules the judges, too." Everyone knew that. But his mild uncle picked the strangest times to be stubborn.

His hands trembled. Strength ruled. Any doubt of that was drowned out by the booming that shook his body into a total state of numbness. He felt nothing in his hands or legs, nor in his mind or heart. Had they deserted him or been frozen by his terrifying surroundings?

A hundred sounds—scrapings and rattlings—bombarded his ears, and he whirled to find their source. Glistening rivulets of moisture ran between crevices in the dark rocks. He thought he heard weeping, as if the stones wept for him. Then he realized the crying came from beyond their walls—from other cells. Though he was exhausted, the cold, cruel air of the prison—broken by the soft sobbing—kept him awake till dawn.

# 8

WHEN HE TRIED to move the next morning, every muscle in his body resisted, aching from a night of lying on the damp straw. Nathan wondered what it would have been like without his blanket. His stomach rumbled. Would they be fed? The chilly question shuddered through him. He prayed they would, but heard no movement in the corridor.

Bridget woke crying, and Edmund whimpering, "I'm cold." Nathan pulled them close and then decided, "Edmund, we must move around to get warm. We have to exercise, or we'll lose all the strength in our muscles." Edmund glanced at his own small arm and nodded agreement.

After they walked around and around, the stiffness gradually left his bones. His right foot still ached, but he forced himself to continue the monotonous circle. Edmund followed him obediently.

"This isn't an adventure," Edmund complained as he suddenly started to cry. "I want to go home!" Nathan lifted his little brother and hugged him.

Awakened by Edmund's sobbing, Uncle Thomas sat up, a dazed expression on his face. "Ellen, I'm so tired," he finally mumbled.

"Go back to sleep, Thomas. . . . We're all right. Nathan, help me slip my blanket under him."

"What's wrong?" Nathan asked.

"He's hurt from the blow he received yesterday. The best we can do is keep him as warm as possible." Nathan watched his mother's hands tremble as he helped her cover Uncle Thomas. She could no longer hide her feelings from them.

Jennett felt her uncle's swollen forehead. "He doesn't feel warm, mother. But my hands are so cold, I can't tell."

"He has no fever, Jennett." She took her daughter's hands and rubbed them briskly. "I pray the fever does not come in this . . . prison." Her voice broke as she forced the word out. "I have nothing to even make a poultice to ease the swelling. We can only pray. . . ."

"What good have prayers done us so far?" Nathan exclaimed. "Prayers will not dissolve these stone walls or help Uncle Thomas!"

His mother stared at him. After a few seconds, she said, "There is nothing left but faith. Don't forget that. The spirit of God within us can provide the strength we need to survive."

A jangling of keys and rattling from the hallway interrupted them. They turned toward the door.

"Hold me up, Nathan," Edmund begged.

The tiny window in the door was closed so they could not see out. Finally, a key was inserted into their lock, and the door groaned open. Jennett backed into a corner with Edmund and the baby while Nathan moved in front of his family.

Old Hal stepped in, carrying a pitcher and bowl from a cart. "Food and water for ye," he announced. Nathan gratefully took the bowl, but his stomach knotted when he saw the contents— lukewarm water with a layer of grease from some probably rotten meat. He did not know if the others could eat or drink the rancid-smelling broth.

"Tomorrow is fresh straw day," Hal reported. "Me wife and me changes the straw for 'em as has a little consideration." He paused. "And maybe a bit of extra food for 'em as shows their thanks. . . ." While the old man waited for a response, Nathan resisted the urge to dump the bowl over his shaggy head.

"I understand," Nathan's mother answered.

"I knew ye would." A smile parted Hal's dirty beard.

"But I must wait until I can speak to my brother," she told him. "As you can see, he is not well today."

79

"Oh." For the first time Hal seemed to notice Uncle Thomas's still form under the blanket.

"Do ye have relatives or friends who will pay? I can get a note to 'em."

"I must wait until I can speak to Thomas," she repeated firmly.

"Certainly, certainly. . . . See you tomorrow." Hal closed the cell door with a clang that echoed in Nathan's ears. For a time, he felt like smashing the bowl against the door. But then he stopped himself. They would receive no other food today.

"Uncle Thomas has money in his coat, mother," Nathan reminded her. "Why don't we give it to the old rat for food?"

"Because, he would take the money and give little in return. I will never tell him the names of our friends; they might also be arrested. . . . We have enough food for a few days, if we are careful. Then Thomas will be better." She tried to speak brightly, but her words seemed false in the putrid air.

Nathan sank helplessly into the straw. He understood her distrust of Hal. In just one day, he hated the old man. "Mother, what can we do?" he asked.

As they gathered around the bowl, mother answered, "Sometimes there isn't anything we can do. We must put the matter in God's hands."

Nathan groaned to himself as he skimmed a layer of grease from the top of the broth with his meat knife. They didn't need speeches from a Quaker meeting now. They needed help.

He decided the best place for the smelly grease was outside their cell. So he climbed up and wiped his knife on the side of the window. With an added bitter thought, he drew the "lucky" hare's foot from his coat and tossed it through the bars with one angry motion.

"I'm hungry," Edmund said as he looked doubtfully at the bowl. "I'll try some."

"Not too much at first, Edmund," their mother cautioned. "Let each one drink a little and save the rest. Cut them small portions of the cooked rabbit we brought, Nathan." The boy insisted his mother eat a piece, too.

"We must hide the rest of our food," she advised. Nathan slipped the rest of the rabbit, some cheese, and apples into his hiding spot. Then they tucked all the books in the blankets, except *Aesop's Fables*, which Jennett read to Edmund. Since Hal said he would not be back until tomorrow, they felt no one would look in their cell.

"The books are safe enough today," mother said, looking into Nathan's hiding spot. "We must save them if we can, Nathan."

"Tonight, I'll make the hole bigger," he promised.

A shadow darkened the small window. Nathan looked up, expecting to see Christopher. But, instead, a tabby cat hovered at the bars, licking the grease. They all noticed the cat at once, but Edmund scrambled up to see. As he reached out to pet the animal, it crawled boldly into the cell, padding lightly down the rocks to the straw.

This black veteran of a thousand battles made a silent, sniffing inspection of their cell. The cat's ears, shredded though they were, stood proudly over a long scar above his eyes. Nathan could see its ribs through the sparse, black fur. Yet the half-grown animal pranced as though he were the most beautiful creature on earth. With a loud purr, he rubbed against each of their legs. Delighted, Edmund picked the cat up, sitting down to smooth its patchy fur. With a long stretch and yawn, the tabby curled up and went to sleep on Edmund's lap.

Booming strains of a bawdy tavern ballad drifted from the alley into their cell. Nathan would have told Christopher to stop singing the shocking words, but he noticed a sparkle of mirth in Jennett's eyes, and a smile briefly part her lips.

Friends believed music too worldly. If this song was an example, Nathan could understand why the Quakers disapproved of it. He had never heard a ballad's words so clearly. His mother, hovering over Thomas, did not seem to hear the singing.

Even the black tabby's ears twitched as the lusty voice neared the cell and stopped. The young guard's face appeared at the bars.

"Good morning, Edmund. Are you there?"

"Hello, Christopher," Edmund replied. "I can't climb up. I have a tabby sleeping on my lap."

"Which one?" Chris asked.

"He's black."

"All black . . . with torn ears?"

"Yes."

"That's King Charles."

"King Charles?"

"Hssh, lad. You must learn to whisper," Christopher cautioned.

"I forgot. Is that really his name?"

"That's the name I gave him. Named him after the king. . . . He's my favorite. There are several who live out here. They usually roam at night and seem to have their own territories. This area belongs to Charles. You're lucky they're here. They keep rats and mice from the cells."

Edmund looked admiringly at the scrawny form in his lap.

"Edmund," Chris whispered. "I have something for you."

"I'll go up, Edmund," Nathan offered, climbing to the window.

Chris smiled broadly. "You're Edmund's brother?"

Nathan nodded.

"How many of you are there?"

"Six." Nathan explained their capture. "We're not guilty of any crime."

"I believe you." Chris pushed a flask into

83

Nathan's hand. "Milk for the babe and Edmund. Our cow has a calf, and more milk than she needs. My mom can't stand the thought of such little ones in prison. She says it's cruel and unfair. . . . Let them drink, and return the flask on one of my rounds by the window."

"Thank you, Christopher." Nathan took the flask, admiring the older boy's muscular arms.

Bridget drank greedily from the flask and screamed when he pulled it from her lips to give Edmund his turn. Outraged, she tried to take it back. But Jennett held her close. Even Nathan swallowed enviously as he watched his brother drink the fresh milk.

When he finished, Edmund glared at Bridget, complaining, "She's waking my cat!"

Nathan climbed up with the flask, waiting for Chris to return from a march down the alley.

"I'll bring more tomorrow," Christopher promised.

"Thank you," Nathan told the guard sincerely. "Someday I'll repay you."

"Of course." Nathan saw the youth smile indulgently. *But I meant what I said,* Nathan thought.

"I'll try to bring more," Chris offered. "But it's difficult for me to hide extra flasks."

"Don't put yourself in danger," Nathan cautioned.

"I already have." Christopher disappeared, booming out another outrageous ballad. What his voice lacked in quality, he made up for in volume. For some reason, the lusty song made Nathan smile, too. He should object to the worldliness of the tune. But he now questioned so many principles of his family's faith that one more doubt was no surprise to him.

As the singing echoed through the alley, Nathan scratched a small mark on one rock. He did not want to lose track of time. If they lost that, Nathan felt he would lose his tie with the outside world.

A whimpering outside the window caused him to look up. There, nuzzling his nose through the bars, was Dog!

Nathan jumped to the window, his heart full of thanks for the faithfulness of this creature they hardly knew. As Nathan reached to stroke Dog's wet nose, the animal dropped the gooey hare's foot on the ground. He pawed the bars, trying to enter the cell some way. Then he whimpered and flopped down by the opening.

"Your dog?" Christopher asked.

"One I found in London," Nathan answered. "He's followed us all this way."

"Something's the matter with his foot—it's bleeding." Christopher reached for the leg, and Dog yelped. But the guard persisted and dug a rock from his paw.

"I'll take care of him," Christopher promised. "We have plenty of meat bones he can eat."

As good as his word, Christopher brought both

milk and bones the next morning. Nathan asked him about the Crispins.

"They're well, but weak," he reported. "I brought them an extra flask, and . . ." Chris pulled a cut of cheese from under his coat and slipped it to Nathan. "I gave them half of this cheese."

"I hope you're thanking the Lord for Christopher's help," Jennett told her brother after he left.

"Of course," he lied, resenting advice from his younger sister.

"I thank the Lord, too, Jennett," their mother added. "Without Christopher's help, the young ones wouldn't survive here."

"Will Uncle Thomas get better, mother?" They both looked over to the corner where Thomas lay wrapped in blankets. Nathan thought he saw movement, a fluttering of his uncle's eyelids, and knelt down to slip his hand under Thomas' restlessly tossing head.

The man opened his eyes.

"What's happened? . . ." his weak voice asked. "What's happened?"

# 9

"THOMAS!" Mother threw her arms around the weak man's neck. Tears choked her efforts to say more.

Jennett grasped his hand. Nathan had felt his uncle would never wake from his semiconscious slumber. But Thomas was tougher than he had realized.

"Oh, my dears." He struggled to sit up. "I've left you alone in this dreadful hole. Forgive me." The three of them helped him sit with his back against the stone wall.

Jennett tenderly slipped his spectacles over his ears.

"Thank you." He pushed the glasses up on his nose and looked around, possibly hoping to find they were not in the filthy prison.

Everyone tried to tell him what had happened at once. Finally, their mother quieted them and told

Thomas about Christopher's help and the jailor's bargaining.

"Fresh straw to replace this filth. . . . Well, we must have it. The Crispins, too," Thomas vowed. Nathan agreed, although he did not think their coins would last long, once Hal caught the scent of money.

He gave Thomas a piece of cheese he had saved in his coat. Then Nathan drew the leftover rabbit out of the hole in the wall. The meat crawled with vermin.

Nathan brushed off the insects, but could not bring himself to eat the meat. He threw the infested rabbit out the window. Dog made certain the rabbit was not wasted by dragging it back near the window and crunching it down in a few bites.

Nathan bit into an apple and then gave it to Edmund. For some reason, the small piece of fruit churned in his stomach and coated his tongue.

His insides still burned the next morning when they helped Thomas stand up. Their uncle walked unsteadily but insisted on climbing up to speak to Christopher. He asked if Chris would buy some parchment. Nathan regretted the fearful waste of coin, even though Chris promised to bring them bread with the leftover money.

Nathan should have known the quill would not be left at home. Uncle Thomas meant to continue his eternal letter writing, even when their keepers planned to let them rot.

"Uncle Thomas, you have no ink," Edmund mentioned after Christopher had returned the next day with the paper and bread. Their uncle horrified them by penning his letter with the juice from smashed bugs. *If he uses the insects, he can write forever.* That thought almost ruined Nathan's pleasure in tasting the first bread he had eaten in days. But now he found that anything was edible if a crust of bread accompanied it.

When Christopher strode back by the window, Thomas offered to pay him to post the letter. For the first time, Christopher hesitated.

"Any food I'm carrying might be for me, and blank parchment . . . for anything. But a letter signed by you would send me to prison, or worse."

"Your letters can't go through the post houses, anyway, uncle," Nathan added. "The king's men can open any letter."

"You're right." Thomas glanced over his message, then looked up. "But if I can get one letter to the right man, we might have a chance. Here we have none."

Nathan noticed Dog stretched out as usual beside their barred window, enjoying the sun. Each night Dog followed Christopher home, begging for bones. Each day he lay there, patiently waiting. As Nathan petted him, his finger caught in the red tie Uncle Thomas had made which still dangled from Dog's neck.

"Hide the parchment in this tie!" he suggested to

Christopher. "Will you do it?" The guard looked straight into Nathan's eyes and nodded.

"Try to hire a rider who is sympathetic to dissenters, Christopher." Thomas placed several coins in the guard's hand. "Thank you for taking such a risk."

Days went by, then weeks. Once, Thomas drew a picture of Bridget's cross and added the jeweler's initials on the back. Maybe he hoped to find a relative who would at least save the baby.

Even with Christopher's help, Nathan realized they would eventually starve. Dreams of plum puddings and roasting fowl drifted to him often. He could smell the aroma from a kitchen hearth and taste the satisfying flavor, bringing saliva to his mouth. In his fantasies, he bit into sweet and juicy apples fresh from the orchard. But the clanking of their cell door often interrupted these dreams, blotting out his delight. That ominous clank renewed his stomach's ache for food.

His gums bled often. Only Edmund and Bridget seemed to be spared this discomfort. The baby fussed as she cut her teeth, wearing her corals down to nothing. They watched her carefully, because she continually wanted to stuff straw in her mouth.

The itching and scratching that engulfed his whole body kept him from concentrating on any one idea for long. Bridget and Edmund screamed as mother picked lice from their skin. Nathan also felt like crying, but he fought back tears and squished any foreign creatures with extraordinary pleasure.

"It's no use. . . . We must . . ." His mother took a knife in her hand one morning and lined them up.

The dull meat knife pulled and hacked at their hair. It hurt Nathan and the little ones. But only Jennett—so good and uncomplaining until that moment—began to sob uncontrollably as her hair disappeared into the matching straw. She cried until Nathan wished he could bury his head in a blanket, blocking the sound and the agony he felt for her.

Even Chris peered in to find out what had happened. "Let me talk to her," he asked. But she refused, backing into a corner and burying her head in her arms. Neither Bridget's and Edmund's hugs nor Thomas's and mother's kind words would console her. Finally, Nathan put his arm around her, gently raising her lowered head.

"I look worse," he told her. "We all look horrible. But your hair will grow back prettier than ever, Jennett . . . prettier than ever." She put her arms around his chest and cried until her wet tears soaked through his coat and shirt. Finally she stopped. Nathan wiped her face. His own frustration made him tremble, for he knew the next time he saw Hal he *would* break that bowl of slop over the greedy jailor's head. His eyes drifted to the cell window to see Christopher staring at them.

91

For the first time, he resented their friendly guard's intrusion on their privacy. *Christopher was free!*

"Go away!" he shouted bitterly, and instantly regretted the words as Chris' face vanished. But Nathan had seen the hurt on the guard's face.

"Nathan." His uncle's harsh tone made him feel even worse. "Have you been taught to speak to others in that manner? Chris is our friend, our only friend here. Consult your conscience."

"I'm sorry, uncle. I will ask Chris to forgive me. . . . But how long can we survive here? Look at these marks." Nathan pointed to the scratches covering the rock—months of confinement in the prison. "We must get out! No answer has come to your letters. We must find another way."

"I shall write until I receive an answer," Thomas asserted. "We are not held in this prison justly."

"What has justice to do with it? We're here," Nathan retorted. "There's no hope, unless we do something before we are too weak to move."

Thomas sighed, walking to the stone wall. He lifted his arms and leaned against the rocks with his head down. No one spoke, for they all respected silence.

As Nathan watched his uncle's unmoving form, he realized the lifeless posture mirrored his own emotions. *He feels the same helplessness I do*, Nathan thought, feeling closer to him than ever before.

Uncle Thomas straightened and turned to mother. As he spoke, the tired, worn ring of his voice vanished, and he talked with a schoolmaster's authority.

"Ellen, I've forgotten to help the children. I cannot allow them to exist here and let their minds grow idle. We will have lessons."

Nathan groaned, wishing he had not complained aloud. "How can we have lessons here?"

"I have my books, and we will use the rocks for writing, if necessary."

"In prison? What can we learn here?"

"Anything you want, Nathan. You are the only person who can imprison your mind."

There was no arguing with him or mother. Every day, they studied. For Uncle Thomas, at least, the dungeon had miraculously become his house in London.

Chris listened whenever he paused on his daily rounds. "You're lucky, Nathan. I cannot read or write." Nathan would have offered to change places, if it had not seemed so ridiculous.

"I'll teach you someday," he promised.

Nathan found that because he could do nothing else, reading gave him pleasure, focusing his mind and transporting him outside the ever present bars. His eyes watered badly as he followed the words, but he did not give up. Soon his skill matched Jennett's.

Little Edmund proudly mastered reading, too.

Even Bridget sat with them every day, fussing because she was not allowed to touch the valuable books.

In the nights, Nathan made small headway into the rock, his mind chasing ideas from books like More's *Utopia*. King Charles, a frequent visitor, stretched flat, waiting patiently for a cockroach to inch out from a crevice in the stones. The cat ate his victim with as much enjoyment as a man gnawing on pigeon bones. Then he would lick his paws and wait again, tail switching, for another unwary bug. When the cat left their cell, Nathan set the debris from his scrapings on his back.

King Charles slipped off into the night, and Nathan turned toward his resting family. He did not understand how they slept when ghosts from the dark corners shattered the blackness with muffled cries, moans, and often scraping. . . . Obviously, others labored with his same plan of escape.

Weary at last, Nathan pulled his blanket around him and sat against a wall to rest and dream. He, his father, and Edmund were fishing and brought their catch home for dinner. The smell of fish cooking made his mouth water, but an eerie cry of "Hello" broke his dream. "HELLLLOOOooo," the spectre whispered. "Please answer me." The plea ended with a sob.

*The lessons continued, even in prison!*

# 10

THE GHOSTLY WORDS traveled from beyond the stones where Nathan rested his head. Uncle Thomas slipped up beside him in the darkness. "Someone from the next cell is speaking to us."

"Matt!" Nathan called happily, but then realized their friends' cell would be on the other side.

"Can you speak to me? What did you say?" the soft, feminine voice asked.

They pinpointed a spot in the wall where the speaking seemed the loudest. The person on the other side must have hollowed the stone, so only a small distance separated them. Why would anyone scrape forever into another cell?

"Shall I dig from this side, uncle?"

"No." Thomas stopped Nathan from going for his hidden knife.

"Don't dig!" the woman warned. "The jailor might notice the hole."

"Why did you tunnel this way?" Thomas questioned the unknown prisoner.

"My sister and I found this hole already begun when we were imprisoned," the voice explained. "I continued to dig when she died, to give myself something to do, some hope."

At first, Nathan refused to admit that people died here. But he knew many probably did. Often he felt the aura of death creeping out of the walls and suffocating him.

"What's your name?"

"Marjory Thompson. I've wanted to talk to someone. That's why I continued to dig. Do you understand?"

"Yes."

"I have nothing else to live for."

"Aren't you well?" Nathan asked.

"Very weak. I can't last much longer," Marjory admitted. "I haven't eaten in two days. Either they think me near death—and not worth bothering about—or they've forgotten me."

Nathan knew any forgetting was on purpose. "Uncle Thomas, I can open the hole and give her food, then replace the opening with a rock."

"Too risky, Nathan. We must find another way." He leaned close to the wall. "Marjory, how did you and your sister come here? Of what are you accused?"

"Treason to the king, the jailor said. My sister and I are of the Quaker faith. That is, she was. . . ."

"We are, too," Nathan told her.

"She and I brought food and clothing to the prisoners. They allowed us in twice. But the third time, they forced us into a cell."

"This foul place!" Uncle Thomas banged the stone wall with his fist, the first show of outrage Nathan had ever seen him make.

"What is it?" Nathan's mother came over and learned of Marjory.

"Do not lose hope," she spoke tenderly to the woman. "We will help you."

"Just speaking to you has helped me. Thank you."

Nathan tried to imagine living alone in that small space for days, months, even years. He would rather die.

"How long have you been here?" he asked.

"I don't know. Months, I think. I sleep a lot now. Nothing else to do, and I'm so weak."

"The jailors have become judges. How many have been wronged?" Thomas asked bitterly, ". . . held without ever going to court. . . . We have lost our rights."

In the morning, Chris agreed to help Marjory. Nathan watched as his uncle put another piece of parchment through the window.

"That was my last coin," Thomas announced glumly. "Well, the books go next."

"No, uncle!" Jennett protested.

"We have no other choice, Jennett. Someday I will replace them."

The day the first book disappeared through the

bars, Jennett cried softly. Would she rather starve? Nathan wondered. The valuable books would bring money for bread. Nathan could only guess how long the books would last. What would they do after that?

Thinking about the future made him uneasy. But some slight hope gave him strength to lift out the large stone at night and dig. Soon moving became difficult. His right foot no longer just ached; it throbbed continually. Often his body said, "Go to sleep. Stay asleep forever." But if he did, he soon woke starving with his head throbbing. His gums became so sore that any bread Chris brought had to be broken in tiny bits and chewed slowly. He recognized that they all became more and more listless. Still, Nathan forced himself to scrape at the solid rock.

"This will take years." He clutched the stub of his worn knife in desperation and almost threw it against the cell wall. In all these months, he had scraped a hole not much bigger than Bridget. Now his knife would not last much longer.

"I won't give up!" When his own knife disintegrated, he would use his uncle's. They had no meat to cut, anyway. Viciously, he attacked the stone again and, to his surprise, buried the short knife into soft dirt! His heart beat like he were running as he drew the knife out and stuck his shaking fingers into the soft clay beyond. As soon as he broke a bigger hole, the digging would be simpler.

"Now Chris will have to help me take the dirt away." He could not get rid of a large amount of dirt as easily as the scrapings.

Smiling, he replaced the rock and wrapped his dirty blanket tightly around him. This new hope helped him sleep. He closed his tired eyes and dozed several hours until late morning.

Because no one stirred in the cell, he woke slowly. Gradually, the excitement of the night returned.

"I must speak to Christopher," he shouted out loud, tossing his blanket into the straw and climbing up the stones. He stared in disbelief. An unfamiliar guard paced the alley. Dog was gone, too.

Nathan dropped back to the floor. "Where can he be?" he muttered aloud. Chris had never been sick.

"Christopher isn't here?" Edmund asked with a bewildered look on his small, white face. His hands clutched the cat tightly, probably fearing the animal might also desert him.

Nathan hated to voice his first thought, "Do you think they found out he helped us?"

Thomas shook his head. "I have no answers, Nathan."

All day, he pulled himself up to the tiny window, praying the new guard would be replaced by their friend. But his hopes never came true. To match Nathan's mood, a cool, drifting fog invaded the alley at night, until their cell was engulfed in a damp haze. His mother and uncle spoke with their heads together, and later they talked to Marjory through the wall. He did not need to hear what they said. Their worried tones told him everything. The strength needed to attack the rock and soil beyond ebbed from him, like the shallowest ocean tide. Jennett held Edmund and Bridget close, so they could sleep as warmly as possible—one blanket under them and two on top. But Nathan's brain refused sleep, so he tucked his own blanket around them tenderly.

"At least be warm tonight, my dears," he said softly. Then Nathan sat shivering against the stones, rubbing his swollen eyes until they burned so he wanted to tear them out. The itching and crawling lice stung his skin, and he held his knotted stomach, wishing he could sleep like the others. How blessed it would be to sleep forever.

"But I'm only twelve years old. I want to live!" he cried out loud. "Tomorrow night I'll have the strength to dig. I'll not die here!"

Sometime in the dawning hours, he dozed. Later he started awake to find himself sitting against the cold wall, covered with four blankets. Jennett, Edmund, and Bridget sat around him.

"Nathan," his sister brushed his forehead lightly with her thin fingers. "You were so cold when I found you this morning. Why did you put your blanket over us?"

"I wanted you to be warm one night, Jennett. I can't rest."

"Well, you were asleep when we found you. Thank you, but don't do that anymore," Jennett insisted. "Once we sleep, we're all right. But you, Nathan. This morning we found you so cold, I feared . . ."

"Don't be afraid, Jennett." He took her hand, remembering that once he held thicker, more rounded fingers. "I will not die here. None of us will. I swear it. I have a plan to escape if only Chris . . ."

"Chris is gone again today," Edmund broke in.

Nathan checked the alley, trying to organize the confused whirl in his mind. Bridget fussed and stuffed straw into her mouth while they all watched and ignored her. Since they had no food, no one had the heart to stop her.

"Listen!" Edmund cried. "The jailor's coming."

"Shall we give him a book to sell?" Nathan asked.

"I want to hold out one more day, Nathan." His uncle rubbed his chin, now covered with a medium-length gray beard that obviously itched fiercely. "Maybe Christopher will return tomorrow."

Hal entered their cell with a bowl of broth Nathan ached to drink. Bridget struggled toward it from Jennett's arms, and Edmund eagerly edged to the bowl.

Hal took Thomas aside. "What can I get for ye this day?"

"I have no more coin," Thomas answered slowly.

The words echoed fatefully in the following silence.

The old man drew in his breath. "Would ye want me to send a note to friends?"

"We probably have no friends to notify outside this prison," Uncle Thomas replied softly.

"Well, think on the matter." Hal turned and looked at them all, one by one. "I don't know when I'll be returnin'."

If Nathan had held his knife, he would have plunged the stubby blade into the jailor's flesh. Every evil in the world seemed to dance in his eyes. *What more could they do to me if I killed him?* Nathan wondered. He hated old Hal, who probably ate more in one day than all of them had eaten in a month. But he fought his desire to attack the jailor the next time he returned . . . if he ever did.

Later in the day, Nathan worried more about Christopher's disappearance than Hal's doubtful return.

"I'm still hungry!" Edmund cried.

Nathan held the little boy for a time and read to him. Then mother held him while he napped. Nathan noticed his brother slept more and more. *Maybe that's best for him.* He envied the small resting form.

If only Christopher's bawdy ballads or smiling face would come back, Nathan would fall on his knees in thankful prayer. But their friend did not appear, so his hopes shrank back to himself and the work he could do alone.

At night, he attacked the stone again. He pulled at the softer soil with his bare, cupped hands, burying the clay under the straw. If Hal did not plan to clean their cell, who would notice?

His uncle and mother spoke to Marjory, encouraging her to hold on. "How I wish we could help her, Ellen," Thomas said as he rested his head against the stones. "Only now, we can't even help ourselves."

"Try to sleep, Thomas. Please rest now, Nathan." His mother slipped her arm around him.

"A little more soil, mother."

"Let him work, Ellen. It gives him hope, and we all need that badly. We must look ahead to better times." As ridiculous as his words sounded, Nathan knew Thomas was sincere.

In the dawning hours, the boy replaced the stone and piled straw around the spot to rest.

"Hello."

Nathan's eyes popped open, and he sprang up at the sound of the familiar voice.

"Chris!" Nathan shouted. They all rushed to the window, trying to speak at once.

"I'm sorry I left you. Here." He held out the familiar flask, a loaf of bread, and cheese. Dog pressed his nose against the bars and wagged his tail eagerly.

"We worried so," Thomas began, breaking the

loaf and cheese in half and handing part back to Chris for Marjory and the Crispins.

"Christopher, we feared for you," Jennett told him.

"My mom got worse . . . and died." The words broke Christopher's usually bright voice. Nathan wanted to reach out to him in some way, but the bars were an impossible barrier. Instead, Nathan prayed for Christopher's kind mother. If only they could have thanked her.

"I came to give you these." Chris's hands thrust two letters between the bars!

# 11

NATHAN WATCHED Uncle Thomas break the wax seal and unfold the parchment with numb disbelief. A low, deep pounding began in his chest as his uncle read. The booming rose, almost drowning his uncle's words.

Dear Friends,

I received the news of your plight and am journeying to court immediately to plead your case. Since you were imprisoned without benefit of a magistrate, the law should favor you. But these are difficult times. If necessary, I will have an audience with the king. Trust in our Lord.

Your friend,<br>
William Penn

Uncle Thomas barely spoke the last words of the

letter. Tears etched a white stream through the dirty grime on his cheeks and disappeared into his gray beard.

"What does it mean?" Edmund looked from his uncle to his mother as she took the message to read herself.

"We're not forgotten, Edmund! Someone outside knows about us." Nathan's voice resounded through the cell. He would have scooped up his little brother and hugged him, but he did not have the strength.

"I've already started to read the other letter, uncle," Jennett revealed, unable to keep her news any longer. "Henry Crispin's alive! William Penn found him in the Fleet Street prison and arranged for his release."

Quickly, they asked Chris to relay the message to Matt and his family. Matt's father alive! A miracle Nathan had never dared hope for.

"The house in London is safe," Jennett continued when everyone was quiet again. "Isaac and Miles are still watching it. The plague has died out, and people have returned to their homes."

Chris reappeared, excited about the joy he had witnessed. "They thought their father was dead. Now even Matt's mother has new life."

Then Jennett began reading the part she had not yet gotten to.

I believe our only hope is to join other Friends in

the New World. The king has granted me a province as payment for an old debt to my father. If your family would like to join this venture, I will accompany you on a ship that sails this fall. The king has granted your freedom, provided you leave the country.

Nathan could not believe the endless writing had saved them. Maybe Uncle Thomas held a sword that was as powerful as the soldier's sharpened metal. Only a different kind of sword, one that spoke softly but with greater force.

"Read the rest, please, Jennett," Nathan urged.

We would like to send some young men earlier to clear land and build homes before the winter months. Henry Crispin has offered to take his son on this first ship. And Isaac Hibbs has mentioned your nephew, Nathan Cowell.

"I'll go anywhere to escape from here," Nathan said aloud. Then Jennett read Penn's last few lines.

Forgive me for the news of this forced exile, but I am sure the provinces will provide limitless opportunities for our young people.

May the peace of God be within you.

Your friend,
William Penn

At last, the pounding in Nathan's chest slowed. But the excitement had exhausted him. He

*Nathan could not believe the endless writing had saved them.*

watched in silence as his mother and Jennett cried softly.

Edmund's small voice questioned, "Does the letter mean we will go home?"

Nathan summoned all his strength and swooped his brother high in the air. "Yes, Edmund!"

"Or to a new home." Christopher added from outside the window. "Will you go on the first ship, Nathan?

"I've seen an ad posted by the Friends," Chris continued. "A man may buy a hundred acres in the new province for five pounds an acre, and be a freeman there!"

Nathan turned to his family. "A hundred acres of land! We will have a farm again!"

"How can I send my son to that wild land alone?" Nathan's mother asked Thomas.

"Ellen, our choices are limited."

"I'm thirteen now, mother, and Jennett is eleven." As he spoke, Nathan realized that almost a year had been lost in this prison. "Henry Crispin and Matt are going, so I won't be alone. Anyway, I'm older than Matt. We can clear land and build shelter for our own farm! Think of it, mother!"

As he spoke, he noticed Chris reappear at the window for a few seconds and then leave to complete his rounds. Nathan looked out the opening and watched their friend's faltering steps. At one point, Chris paused and glanced back at them. A quiet Chris made Nathan feel uneasy.

"I must write an answer," Thomas said as he drew the worn, split quill from its hiding place in the wall.

"Uncle Thomas." Nathan cleared his throat.

"Yes, Nathan."

"May I write the letter this time?"

Thomas looked surprised, but gave him the quill.

Nathan thought carefully as he composed his message. *The power in this worn feather has released us from prison.* He only asked his uncle one question, "Will the colony be just for Quakers?"

"No, Nathan. All will be welcome there. Many different peoples have already journeyed to the New World for many different reasons, and natives called Indians inhabit parts of the land. We will all have to live together in peace for the new land to be a home."

Nathan thought of Christopher as he wrote. His friend had no one, now that his mother was dead. He had never wanted to guard an alley and these prison walls. He had wanted great adventure, like that in the new land. Maybe Chris was glum because soon they would be living his dream. Nathan mentioned Chris in his letter.

Christopher had always sealed their parchment, so Nathan gave it to him, saying, "You may read this if you wish."

Without replying, their friend rolled the letter into Dog's red collar. Nathan noticed his cheeks

111

were as red as his hair when he turned to continue his rounds. Chris's unusual silence disturbed Nathan all day. No melody boomed through the alley. That quiet, most prized by the Quakers, was unnatural for his friend. Nathan hoped Chris would read the letter and say something the next morning.

But, in the morning, when Chris brought them milk and boiled eggs, he only said hello. Nor did he sing at all that day.

Several times Nathan tried to speak to him, and then he gave up, sinking back against the damp wall to rest. The good news helped him fight the consuming tiredness that invaded his body. He sank back to dream, and this time, not of food.

One morning, Nathan woke to the familiar singing, amazed at how his heart was lifted by the bellowing notes. This singing was all of the prison Nathan would miss, and their friend half yelled his songs.

"Nathan, Nathan!" Edmund cried. "Someone's coming!" No one had come near them in days, so Nathan tensed when he heard the key scraping as it turned. His hopes fell when old Hal stepped into the cell.

Then, two other men appeared behind him. One man, dressed in black velvet royals, examined them with piercing eyes. The other wore a Quaker suit of particularly fine cloth and a wig, unusual for a man of their faith.

112

Thomas almost leaped forward, but he checked himself.

Then the words Nathan had only heard in the other land of his dreams were spoken; words they had all prayed for.

"You are free to go."

But they were unable to respond, to voice the emotion they felt. Finally, Uncle Thomas rushed to the man in Quaker clothes, embracing him. "Thank you, William."

"Thomas, I thank you for telling me of the plight of our friends in this prison."

"We've found most of the prisoners were locked up without being sentenced by a magistrate." Their rich visitor turned toward Hal. "And those responsible must answer for that injustice."

Hal's eyes opened wide as he backed toward the door. "I just followed orders from the captain, sir!"

"Quiet!" the man ordered. He moved in front of Jennett and stood before her, staring at the baby. Bridget clung to Jennett.

"Jen-na!" she shrieked, burying her face in Jennett's filthy, ragged dress. The man reached out to grasp the baby's jeweled cross.

Hal gasped. If he had ever dreamed she wore such a treasure, he would probably have stolen the precious symbol. Even in the dim cell, the stones embedded in the gold glimmered and sparkled.

Without a word, the man dropped the cross and walked around the small cell, examining every inch with his sharp, black eyes. "The stench," he muttered between clenched teeth. "My animals are treated better." He motioned for his servants who were standing in the corridor to take Hal.

Then he turned to Nathan. "Young Friend, what do you suggest I do with this man?" Nathan thought of every cruel act Hal had done to them, which had been repeated a hundred, perhaps a thousand, times to all the other prisoners. He hesitated, then said, "His crimes must be spoken before a magistrate."

"And if you were judge?" The man forced Nathan to suggest some punishment.

"I can think of nothing worse than to be here."

"A just decision. I doubt if I would be as fair in your place. Friend Penn, I promise I will work for a declaration of tolerance for all religions."

The man slipped his hand into his cloak and drew out an object Nathan could not see. "For the sister of the baby," he said, and turned swiftly, disappearing into the corridor.

Nathan could not understand why this man— who must be related to Bridget, or might even be her father—would leave her with strangers, especially Quakers who could not remain in England. The man had the fine features and bearing of a member of the court. Maybe of royalty, Nathan thought, as he remembered the royal coat of arms etched on the silver flask.

He drew close to his uncle, who stood looking at

the object the stranger had given him. A duplicate of Bridget's cross sparkled in his dirty hand. Thomas slipped the necklace over Jennett's shorn head.

"You are free to go," William Penn repeated.

Slowly, they moved out the door, each one of them hesitating at the archway that led to the floor above. Matt and Mary Crispin greeted them with hugs. Nathan saw Henry Crispin standing beside them.

Every step up made Nathan's heart work harder. Finally, he had to stop, breathing heavily. He knew he should run up. But he had to force his body to move—up . . . up . . . one endless step at a time, telling himself that at last he would be out.

William Penn told Nathan, Matt, and Henry Crispin that they would rest at his home before sailing to Pennsylvania. The others would return to London. Marjory Thompson would go with them, because she had no one else. She looked mercilessly thin, and her skin and hair were the same color of gray. Nathan thanked the Lord he could not see himself. He nodded to all the conversations that jumbled around him, desperately trying to gasp air through his mouth and nose.

An explosion of light forced his body back when the huge iron door of the prison opened to give them their freedom.

Now he should shout for joy. He had held back a scream for so long! But no amount of effort would bring sound from his throat. Nathan squinted to see the walking ghosts that were his family. They all looked like thin, dirty mice dragged from a hole. He could not tell if his uncle's hair was coated with grime or was actually gray. And his mother . . . his once beautiful, blond mother . . .

Probably the bright light blinded him, shocking him into an ironlike statue. Nathan's feet, now free, should run. But instead, they felt like tree roots attached to the ground. He knew they must move toward William Penn's carriage, but his knees began to wobble and the brilliant sunlight stabbed into his throbbing head. He groped for support, reaching out for Christopher. Strange that he would imagine someone who was not a Quaker would help him. . . . But it could not be Christopher, because the boy did not wear a uniform.

Slowly, Nathan focused his eyes on the figure beside him. It was Christopher! "What are you doing here?" he mumbled. "Where is your uniform?"

"I'm going to the New World with you," Christopher replied, smiling his familiar wide grin.

"To Pennsylvania?" Nathan tried to concentrate on the meaning of Chris's words.

"Yes, I've sold my home and cow. I'll farm a hundred acres," his voice boomed happily. "And be a freeman there, like the rest of you."

The last of Christopher's words sunk into the

whirlpool that pulled Nathan deeper into blackness.

"Help!" Christopher's voice shouted. Someone braced Nathan's elbows and helped Chris get him into the waiting carriage. He lay back into the soft, plush cushions and slept peacefully as they rode away from the prison.

# The Wonderful World of Picture Strip Books

The Adventures of Tullus, teenage Christian in ancient Rome. Tullus fights for his faith against the terrors of his time. Exciting adventures in black-and-white picture strips, with fast-moving dialogue! Each book 112 pages.

**Tullus and the Ransom Gold.** Can Tullus find enough money to free his Christian friends from death in the arena? He does —but then finds himself in the arena . . . defending a girl from a savage lion. What can he do! 77057—$1.25

**Tullus and the Vandals of the North.** Go with Tullus as he explores the outer limits of the ancient Roman empire . . . see how faith and prayer help him turn trials into opportunities to win others for Christ. 81249—$1.25

**Tullus and the Kidnapped Prince.** Would you risk your life for a savage young prince in faraway India? Tullus does. See why! 84152—$1.25

**Tullus in the Deadly Whirlpool.** Can Tullus convince the sailors he's not to blame for the storm and whirlpool that threaten their ship? He must convince them. But how? 77065—$1.25

Boxed gift set of 4 books. $4.95

**Christian Family Classics.** Two famous stories—"Ben Hur," and "Christian Family Courageous." Learn how a youth in Bible times overcame tremendous adversity. Read how a shipwrecked family provided for its needs on a tropic island. Both stories told in black-and-white picture strips, dialogue, captions. 81786—$1.25

Handy order form on last page

# The Wonderful World of Teen Paperbacks

**Never Miss A Sunset.** Put yourself in Ellen's place: 75 years ago, on a backwoods farm in Wisconsin. Ellen is 13. She loves her family, but resents being second mother to her nine brothers and sisters. Then tragedy brings Ellen a guilt heavier than all her chores —a terrible burden that remains until winter warms into spring . . . to bring a time of new understanding for Ellen and her mother.                86512—$1.95

**City Kid Farmer.** Won first prize in David C. Cook's 1975 children's book contest! You'll sympathize with Mark; he has to give up his friends when his folks move to the country. But worse, his aunt and uncle are just as "religious" as his mother. You'll see how Mark adjusts to rural life . . . and the chain of events that leads him to know Christ himself.           89474—$1.25

**Pounding Hooves.** More than an exciting horse story— it's the story of Lori's jealous struggle with her friend Darlene. Darlene probably will win the art contest. She'll win Ken, too—Darlene's so pretty! And Storm, the beautiful Arabian stallion—Darlene's father surely will buy him before Lori saves enough money. Rivals for so much . . . even with God's help, can Lori overcome her jealousy of Darlene?           89458—$1.75

**Captured!** Teenage adventure in wilderness America! Captured by Indians, Crist and Zack strike a bargain. The Indians want to learn more about the white man's ways, so the boys agree to teach the Indians—if they will spare their lives. But the boys would rather return home. Why, then, does Crist pass up a chance to escape? And Zack—why does he escape . . . then act so strangely when he finds the chief's son wounded, and helpless?           87312—$1.50

Handy order form on last page

# The Wonderful World of Teen Paperbacks

**Fire!** You'll find mystery in this tale of Ann and Rob, who spend a summer with their aunt and forest-ranger uncle. They look forward to adventure, but they find more than they really want. Can the two teenagers help discover who is starting the forest fires? More important, can they help lead their unbelieving uncle to a greater discovery?                82974—$1.25

**Tanya and the Border Guard.** Tanya lives in Russia, where visible Christians are often persecuted. When her family and friends worship, they must gather secretly in a forest. Was Tanya wise to reveal their meeting place to the soldier, even though he did say he was a believer? She'll soon find out—because now he and two more soldiers appear at their little meeting in the forest!                75994—$1.25

**Alexi's Secret Mission.** For Christian activities, Alexi's family is banished to Siberia. Alexi has to give up his friends; worse yet, he can't be on the school team because he's a Christian. He almost resents his faith! But soon he's involved in something more exciting than sports—spreading God's Word. And what does that service to God bring him? Read fast!    87338—$1.25

**Turkey Red.** When Martha's farming family came to America for religious freedom, they brought a special variety of wheat—red wheat. It grew well in Kansas, but no one would buy red wheat. Brother Jake had other troubles: prairie fires, rattlesnakes, Indians; so he ran away to the city. And for Martha . . . a real problem of the time: should she mix with children who didn't belong to their church? Important lessons in sharing!                89482—$1.25

Handy order form on last page

# The Wonderful World of Children's Books

**❝** Reading about a character is a lot different than seeing him on TV. You can get to know him better—get more deeply involved with him as a person—in a book, because you're with him a lot longer. **❞**

Barbara Reeves, consultant to "Sesame Street"

**IN GRANDMA'S ATTIC.** Ever explore an attic? It's lots of fun—especially when the strange items one finds cause grandma to tell neat stories about the olden days. Fifty years ago, in a big farm house in Michigan, a girl used to explore her grandma's attic . . . and ask questions about the strange things she found. The stories her grandma told are in this book: how a beaded basket led to a scary adventure with a hungry Indian . . . the time grandma took a dare, and nearly froze her tongue on the new pump . . . why grandpa was so positive the shoes a neighbor offered him would fit, because "when the Lord sends me shoes, he sends the right size."
77271—$1.25

Handy order form on last page

# The Wonderful World of Children's Books

**THE SHAWL OF WAITING**
Maybe you'd have done the same, if your grandmother had told you such a strange story. Anyway, after hearing her grandma's story, Emilie Coulter started to knit her own "shawl of waiting." Emilie knit, and knit—even if she didn't believe her grandma's story. But the more Emilie knit, the smaller the shawl became! Why couldn't she finish it?                    89466—$1.25

## Order below